THE SCORPION GOD

When William Golding was awarded the Nobel Prize
in Literature, the Nobel Foundation said of his novels
that they 'illuminate the human condition in the world of
today'. Born in Cornwall in 1911, Golding was educated
at Marlborough Grammar School and Brasenose College,
Oxford. Before becoming a writer, he was an actor, a lec-
turer, a small-boat sailor, a musician and a schoolteacher.
In 1940 he joined the Royal Navy and saw action against
battleships, submarines and aircraft, and also took part in
the pursuit of the *Bismarck*.

Lord of the Flies, his first novel, was rejected by several
publishers and one literary agent. It was rescued from the
'slush pile' by a young editor at Faber and Faber and published in 1954. The book would go on to sell several million
copies; it was translated into 35 languages and made into a
film by Peter Brook in 1963. He wrote eleven other novels,
The Inheritors and *The Spire* among them, a play and two
essay collections. He won the Booker Prize for his novel
Rites of Passage in 1980, and the Nobel Prize in Literature
in 1983. He was knighted in 1988. He died at his home in
the summer of 1993.

www.william-golding.co.uk

Books by
Sir William Golding
1911–1993
Nobel Prize in Literature

Fiction

LORD OF THE FLIES

THE INHERITORS

PINCHER MARTIN

FREE FALL

THE SPIRE

THE PYRAMID

THE SCORPION GOD

DARKNESS VISIBLE

THE PAPER MEN

RITES OF PASSAGE

CLOSE QUARTERS

FIRE DOWN BELOW

TO THE ENDS OF THE EARTH

(comprising *Rites of Passage, Close Quarters* and *Fire Down Below* in a
revised text; foreword by the author)

THE DOUBLE TONGUE

Essays

THE HOT GATES

A MOVING TARGET

Travel

AN EGYPTIAN JOURNAL

Plays

THE BRASS BUTTERFLY

LORD OF THE FLIES

adapted for the stage by Nigel Williams

WILLIAM GOLDING: A CRITICAL STUDY OF THE NOVELS

by Mark Kinkead-Weekes and Ian Gregor

WILLIAM GOLDING

The Scorpion God

Three Short Novels

faber and faber

The Scorpion God and *Clonk Clonk* first published in 1971
by Faber and Faber Limited
Bloomsbury House, 74–77 Great Russell Street,
London WC1B 3DA

Envoy Extraordinary first published in 1956 in *Sometime Never*
by Eyre and Spottiswoode Limited

First Faber paperback edition 1973
This paperback edition first published in 2013

Typeset by Faber and Faber Ltd

Printed and bound by CPI Group (UK) Ltd, Croydon, CR0 4YY

© William Golding, 1956, 1971

Introduction © Craig Raine, 2013

The right of William Golding to be identified as author of this work has been
asserted in accordance with Section 77 of the Copyright, Designs and Patents
Act 1988

A CIP record for this book is available from the British Library

ISBN 978–0–571–29849–5

FSC
www.fsc.org
MIX
Paper from
responsible sources
FSC® C101712

2 4 6 8 10 9 7 5 3 1

Contents

Introduction by Craig Raine

Three novellas set in the irretrievable past. *Clonk Clonk* is a comedy which recovers for us a radically counter-intuitive primitive African society in which women amiably connive in the myth of masculinity. The male hunters in the story are necessary for procreation, but little else, since their society is amply provided for with vegetarian food sources. The women are pragmatically focused on childbirth, on biological necessity, while the men are fickle, effeminate, faintly hysterical and definitely daunted by gynaecology and female sexual mystery. *Envoy Extraordinary* is about premature invention—of gunpowder, of the steam engine, of the pressure cooker—rather like Kipling's story, 'The Eye of Allah', in which the microscope is discovered, only to be suppressed as premature. *The Scorpion God* is about a society predicated on a profound theological error, a metaphysical absurdity—in which one outsider, the Liar, is endangered by his superior knowledge. The measure of the shared short-sightedness is that they take the Liar's truths—about icebergs, about snowflakes—as titillating, as poetic or as jocose fictions, as a kind of magic realism.

'Mountains that wear a white cloak.' 'White mountains floating in water.'

In 1963, Bill Brandt photographed Alberto Giacometti's left eye, eyelid and eyebrow in black-and-white close-up. It looks like fissured mud with a few stiff dead reeds. I thought of it as I re-read the first page of *The Scorpion God*: 'The flocks of river birds that stood where the mud of the river bank was hard and shattered with hexagonal cracks looked colourfully at nothing. The beds of dry papyrus—slashed with the occasional stem that had bent, broken and leaned against the others—were still as reed-beds *painted in a tomb*, except when a seed toppled out of a dried crown . . .' (my italics).

The very first sentence tells us, strangely, 'There was not a crack in the sky, not a blemish on the dense blue enamel.' We wouldn't expect the sky to be *cracked* unless it were a work of art, a representation of reality in, say, blue faience—Egyptian faience, a ceramic with a high finish, not made of clay—like something 'painted in a tomb'.

Golding's description is not only brilliant—as always— it is also proleptic. This is a story about the Egyptian custom of surrounding mummified pharaohs with clay models of their retinue and servants, their whole way of life. You can see these charmingly detailed painted terra-cotta Playpeople in the Egyptian Museum at Cairo. In his story, however, Golding proposes something more chilling—the entombment of actual retainers, not their miniaturised models. Real life has to enter the tomb—as a replica of itself. The hypothesis is more likely if actual reality is already like a work of art—a still life, a *nature morte*, already a representation of itself. It is already halfway there.

I also thought of Brandt's photograph of Giacometti's eye because it is the perfect image for a technique crucial to Golding's art—the technique of rigorously occluded close-up. So much of Golding's greatest work depends on the severely restricted view, the idea of confinement, of solipsism. Think of the unexpected long shot at the close of *Lord of the Flies* in which we suddenly see the murderous, cruel Jack as 'a little boy who wore the remains of an extraordinary black cap on his red hair and who carried the remains of a pair of spectacles at his waist'. A *little* boy. Suddenly, the 'true' perspective, a different scale—no longer in frightening close-up. Think of *The Spire* and the way Golding locks his narrative into the consciousness of Jocelin, the way everything is focalised from his viewpoint. Think of *Pincher Martin* and the way we share Pincher's deluded fight for survival, immersed in a subjective extended struggle that actually lasts for only a few moments on a different, 'true' scale.

Scale: consider that seed *toppling* out of a dried crown. The verb is exceptional, a great alteration of scale, like Robert Frost's 'sturdy seedling with arched body' (in 'Putting in the Seed')—'Shouldering its way and shedding the earth crumbs.' Only large things can be toppled—kings, governments, temples, pillars, slabs of stone. You can't topple a crumb off a tablecloth. So, when a *seed* topples from a *crown*, the reader succumbs to Golding's imperious magnification. We can't get far enough back, far enough away, to see things as they actually are.

And this is Golding's point. In these three historical novellas—one set in ancient Egypt, one in primitive Africa, one in ancient Rome—he is concerned to enforce the qualia of history, to bring the picture to painful life, to animate the long ago, to make us taste the tannins, experience the enzymes of a vanished time. He rubs our noses in it. Until, at last, he pulls back and allows us to lift our gaze. The Liar's contemptuous epitome: 'A patch of land no bigger than a farm—a handful of apes left high and dry by the tide of men.' Or the long view at the end of *Clonk Clonk*: 'The mountain did not erupt for a hundred thousand years; and though the eruption overwhelmed the spa that had grown up round the Hot Springs, by that time there were plenty of people in other places, so it was a small matter.'

Henry James didn't believe in historical fiction. On 5 October 1901, he writes to his friend, the historical novelist, Sarah Orne Jewett: 'You may multiply the little facts that can be got from pictures & documents, relics & prints, as much as you like—the *real* thing is almost impossible to do, & in its absence the whole effect is as nought; I mean the invention, the representation of the old *consciousness*, the soul, the sense, the horizon, the vision of individuals in whose minds half the things that make ours, that make the modern world were non-existent.' This is the crux of James's objection—that the past is another planet *where people think differently.* 'You have to *think* [i.e. invent] with your modern apparatus a man, a woman,—or rather fifty—whose own thinking was intensely-otherwise conditioned.' James's argument seems plausible.

Except that Golding's speciality is the very area deemed 'impossible' by Henry James—lost ways of thinking, lost ways of feeling, the whole atrophied consciousness of the past. He is an archeologist of the mind's ruined circuits.

So how plausible *is* James's hypothesis? Robert Browning's Duke in 'My Last Duchess', for example, is a Renaissance aristocrat, so confident of his breeding and unassailable status that he can tell an envoy, in his court to arrange a marriage, that he, the Duke, has had his previous wife murdered—for seeming to stoop, for being friendly, for being insufficiently haughty. It isn't an obviously modern democratic cast of mind. He isn't, however, a freak. Strangely, we understand him. Browning gets inside him imaginatively. And, if the Duke is extreme, he isn't unknown, or off the human spectrum. At the conclusion of the poem, he draws the attention of the envoy to a piece of sculpture, Neptune taming sea-horses, cast in bronze by Claus of Innsbruck. It is an emblem of absolute power. It is also a paradox the twentieth century is familiar with—the conjunction of aesthetic connoisseurship with affectless cruelty. Who was it pointed out the proximity of Goethe's Weimar court to the concentration camp at Buchenwald? In Steven Spielberg's film *Schindler's List*, we were given the Hollywood version as two German soldiers paused in their search of the Lodz ghetto to play Schubert on a piano.

Henry James (like Jonathan Franzen in his commencement address to Kenyon College in 2011) believes that inventions, technological advances, improved transport and infrastructure, the BlackBerry, the typewriter, the word-processor, as it were—what Matthew Arnold dismissed as mere externals, as 'machinery'—will change the ways we think. In trivial ways, they will. Fundamentally, however, human beings remain unchanged. When the anthropologist Paul Ekman went in the late fifties to the isolated stone-age Highlanders of New Guinea, he discovered they could recognise the emotions expressed in photographs of contemporary Americans. They were able to make up stories about them. Without this shared pool of unaltered, unalterable feelings, we would not be able to understand the literature of the past.

The Scorpion God, the great masterpiece of these three novellas, shows us that human nature is unchanging even under an imperious theological construct. For example, incest between father and daughter, between daughter and brother, is seen as proper, as right. In this bizarre society, where sex between unrelated strangers is seen as a perversion, nature nevertheless asserts itself. The very idea of sex between strangers is exciting and arousing.

As Pretty Flower explains to the Head Man, the sense of transgression adds edge to the sexual act.

Nevertheless, for practically the whole of this novella Golding emphasises the differences, maximises the apparently insuperable barriers between this primitive society and our own. T. S. Eliot in his introduction to Kipling's verse says that Kipling interests him because Kipling's mind is so very different from his own. Different, yes; unintelligible, no. How is it achieved, this simultaneous assertion of radical difference and essential identity? In Browning's case, he invents idiolects for his historical characters. The physician Karshish is given a medical inflection to his thought and speech. Fra Lippo Lippi's monologue is garnished with archaic exuberances— 'zooks' and so forth. This is partly Golding's method, too. In *Clonk Clonk*, the Skywoman (aka the moon) is a convincing inflection of normality. The idea of 'the Now' in *The Scorpion God*—an eternal fixity or an anxious flux—is idiosyncratic shorthand, an abbreviated idiolect for a whole community's peculiar thought processes. And a brilliant invention.

In Borges's story 'Tlön, Uqbar, Orbis Tertius', the inhabitants of Tlön all believe the material world disappears when no one is perceiving it. When an ur-materialist tries to articulate the idea that reality survives even if it is not perceived, Borges wonderfully, exactly captures the difficulty of articulating, of thinking through a new idea. This is the parable of the coins. 'On Tuesday, X crosses a deserted road and loses nine copper coins. On Thursday, Y finds in the road four coins, somewhat rusted by Wednesday's rain. On Friday, Z discovers three coins in the road. On Friday morning, X finds two coins in the corridor of his house.' From this, the continuity of the coins' existence is asserted. 'It is logical to think that they have existed—at least in some secret way, hidden from the comprehension of men—at every moment of those three periods.' The combination here—of absurdity and of wonky logic—rests on something fundamentally human, which is the difficulty of un-thinking a settled idea. Borges gives us a spare paradigm, the exposition of a concept. Golding, though, can persuade you that you are actually there. In Borges, it is an abstract, intellectual demonstration, elegant and pleasing. In Golding it is the experience itself, in 4-D. You feel it in all its claustrophobic close-up. And you know that Henry James was wrong—because every detail in Golding is imaginatively right.

THE SCORPION GOD

There was not a crack in the sky, not a blemish on the dense blue enamel. Even the sun, floating in the middle of it, did no more than fuse the immediate surroundings so that gold and ultramarine ran and mingled. Out of this sky, heat and light fell like an avalanche so that everything between the two long cliffs lay motionless as the cliffs themselves.

The river water was flat, opaque, dead. The only suggestion of movement anywhere was in the trace of steam that rose from the surface. The flocks of river birds that stood where the mud of the river bank was hard and shattered with hexagonal cracks looked colourfully at nothing. The beds of dry papyrus—slashed with the occasional stem that had bent, broken and leaned against the others—were still as reedbeds painted in a tomb, except when a seed toppled out of a dried crown; and where a seed fell on the shallows, there it lay and did not stir. But farther out the water was deep—must be miles deep for the sun burned down there too and fused the blue enamel of an undersky that matched the heavy blue vault above the red and yellow cliffs. And now, as if two suns were more than they could bear, the cliffs half hid themselves behind the air and began to shake.

Between the cliffs and the river, the black earth was burnt up. The stubble seemed as little like life as the feathers caught everywhere among the separate stubs. The few trees, palms, acacias, hung down their foliage as if they had given up. The houses of limewashed mud seemed as alive as they and not more motionless; not more motionless than the men and women and children who stood on either side of a beaten track that lay parallel with the river and an easy stone's throw from the bank. These people were all looking away down river, away from the sun which made short, cobalt shadows at their feet. They stood over their shadows and looked down river, hands raised a little, eyes unblinking, mouths open.

There was a faint noise down river. The waiting men looked at each other, rubbed sweaty palms on their linen kilts, then held them up, palms outward and even higher than before. The naked children began to call out and run round until the women bent down in their long robes of linen girt above the breast and shook them into silence and stillness.

A man came into sight on the track from the shadow of a group of palms. He moved in somewhat the same way as the shuddering cliffs. Even at this distance it was easy to distinguish him from the scattering of other figures by the strangeness of his dress and by the fact that they were all looking at him. He came to an open patch of stubble and now it was possible to see that he was running, jogging along, bumping up and down, while the groups he passed gesticulated, cried out, and clapped their hands as they kept their eyes on him. He reached a nearer field and his costume came clear and strange as his movements. He wore a kilt and tall hat both of white linen. There were gleams of gold and blue from his sandals, his wrists and from the wide pectoral that was bouncing on his chest; more gleams from the crook and flail he held in either hand. There was a general gleam from his dark skin, where the sweat ran off him and fell on the cracked earth. The people shouted louder when they saw the sweat fall. Those who had run a little way with him, wiped off their own sweat, slackened their pace and let the runner get away from their land.

Now the runner was so near he could be seen in detail. His face had been oval once, but good living and authority had slabbed it to a rectangle in keeping with his stocky body. He looked like a man who had few ideas but held those he had without examining them; and just now, his idea was to run and keep running. But there were outliers to this central idea, outliers of astonishment and indignation. The indignation was reasonable enough, for the linen hat fell every now and then over one eye and the runner would jab at it with the crook. The strings of the flail were made of alternate blue and gold beads and if he lifted it too high they flicked him in the face. Now and then, as if he had reminded himself of something, he would

5

cross the crook and flail before his stomach so that the requirements of running made him rub one on the other as though he were sharpening a knife. All this, and the swarms of flies, were enough to account for his indignation, though the source of his astonishment could not be detected so easily. He came thudding across the field, with now no more than one runner near him—a lean and muscular young man who shouted mixed encouragement, prayer and praise.

"Run, Great House! Run for my sake! Life! Health! Strength!"

As the two men approached the nearer side of the field it was as if they crossed an invisible boundary. The people grouped by the few houses moved forward and began to shout.

"God! God! Great House!"

All at once they were voluble as the young man and tumultuous. They welcomed the runner with shouts and laughter tears. The women hurried to stand in his path and the children were forgotten among the quick, dark feet. He came jogging through the little street and men began to run with him. There was a blind man, thin and knotted as the stick that supported him, who stood with one hand lifted and looked in the general direction of the runner with eyes as white as balls of quartz; but who cried out none the less.

"Life! Health! Strength! Great House! Great House! Great House!"

Then the runner was away again and beyond the hamlet, having drawn the young men with him while the women were left laughing and crying.

"Did you see, Sister? I touched Him!"

But Great House was still trotting on, still jabbing with his crook at the uneasy hat, still indignant and if anything, even more plainly astonished than before. There were few who ran with him now and none from farther back than the hamlet, except the lean young man. After a while even these stopped, breathless but smiling, as Great House and his attendant ran away from them in front of his dancing tail. There was no noise but deep breathing and the thud of receding feet. The men strolled back to the hamlet where the thick beer was being brought out in jars and jugs and dishes to trestles in the crowded street.

When the runner was out of hearing, the blind man who had stood so long by the track lowered his hand. He did not join the crowd in the hamlet. He turned, felt his way with his stick across some stubble, then through a mass of undergrowth until he came to bare mud in the shade of palms where the mud hexagons of the river bank began. A little boy sat in the shade, cross-legged, hands slack in his lap, head lowered, so that the single lock of hair left by the razor fell past his ear to his knee. He was thin as the blind man, though not so dark-skinned; and his kilt was brilliantly clean except where the twigs and dust of the foreshore clung to it.

7

The blind man spoke to the air.

"Well. He is gone. We shall not see that sight for another seven years."

The boy answered listlessly.

"I saw nothing."

"The young man, the one they call the Liar ran with him. He talked all the time."

The boy started up.

"You should have told me!"

"Why?"

"I would have gone to see!"

"The Liar, rather than the God, your Father?"

"I love him. He tells me lies that take away the weight of the sky. And he is."

"Is what?"

The boy spread his hands.

"He just is."

The blind man lowered himself to the ground and laid his stick across his knees.

"It is a great day, little Prince. You knew that, surely?"

"My nurses told me, so I ran away. A great day means standing in the sun and keeping still. Then I am sick. I have to have smokes made and words said. I have to eat things, wear things, drink things."

"I know. Who does not? Your walk sounds like the walk of a little old man. But today the God proves Himself and perhaps you will be better."

"How can He prove Himself?"

8

The blind man thought for a while.

"If it comes to that, how can He keep the sky up and make the river rise? But He does. The sky is there, kept up; and the river will rise as it has risen before. These are mysteries."

The Prince sighed.

"I am tired of mysteries."

"We live by them," said the blind man. "I will show you. Do you see that palm tree on your left?"

"The sun is too bright."

"Well then. If you were to look, you would see notches cut in the trunk. An arm's length from the root is the Notch Of Sorrow. If the water were to rise no farther than that, men would starve. How old are you? Ten? Eleven? When I was not much older than you, it happened so and the God of that time took poison."

"People starved? They died?"

"Men, women and children. But the God is strong, a great lover—though He has no children but your sister and you—a great hunter, eater, drinker. The water will creep up the trunk to the Notch Of Excellent Eating."

The Prince was interested, despite the sun.

"Why is there a notch right at the top?"

The blind man shook his head forebodingly.

"It was prophesied once, I cannot tell when. The notch was made by a God, they say, and the water has never reached it. Too much is worse than too little. The whole world would be drowned and the waters would lap at the

9

House of Life. That is called—" He bent sideways and whispered—"the Notch Of Utter Calamity."

The Prince said nothing and after a moment the blind man fumbled then patted his knee.

"This knowledge is too high for you. Let it be. One day, when I am gone and the God has entered his Now in the House of Life you will be a God yourself. Then you will understand."

The Prince cried out, his head lifted in grief and urgency.

"I don't want to be a God!"

"What's this? Who else is there?"

The Prince beat the dry mud feebly with his fists.

"I won't! They shan't make me!"

"Quietly, child! If they were to hear you—have you no thought for me?"

But the Prince was staring into the white eyes as if he could force them to see him.

"I won't—I can't. I can't make the river rise or keep the sky up—I have dreams—there is darkness. Things falling. They press, they weigh. I can't move or breathe——"

The tears were trickling down the Prince's face. He snivelled and smeared one arm across his nose.

"I don't want to be a God!"

The blind man began to talk loudly and firmly as if to force the Prince to listen.

"When you are married to your Royal Sister——"

"I'm not going to be married, ever," said the Prince

with sudden passion. "Not ever. Especially not to Pretty Flower, but not ever. If I play with boys they want to play at hunting and I get out of breath. If I play with girls they want to play at being married and I have to bounce up and down on them till I get out of breath all over again and then they bounce up and down until I get giddy."

The blind man was silent for a while.

"Well," he said at last. "Well."

"I should like to be a girl," said the Prince. "A pretty girl with nothing to do but be pretty and wear pretty things. Then they couldn't turn me into a God."

The blind man scratched his nose.

"Not keep the sky up? Not make the river rise? Not slay a bull or shoot at a mark?"

"I could never see the mark, let alone hit it."

"What can you mean, child?"

"I have a kind of white smoke in my eyes."

"Prince—are you telling the truth?"

"It grows thicker. Slowly, but thicker."

"No!"

"So you see——"

"But Prince, poor child—what do they say?"

"I have told no one. I am tired of spells and smells and filthy things to drink. I am tired."

The blind man's voice ran up.

"But you will go blind! Little by little, year by year—child! Think of us! Think of the Notch Of Utter Calamity!"

11

"What has it to do with me? If I were a girl———"

The blind man was scrabbling with his stick and feet.

"They must know. He must know at once—poor Prince, poor weak one. Poor people!"

The boy laid hold of the blind man's ankle who pulled himself away and stood up unhandily.

"Don't tell anyone!"

"I must, poor child. They will cure you———"

"No!"

"I shall call out to the God at the end of His run and He will hear me!"

"I don't want to be a God!"

But the blind man was hurrying, tapping with his stick at the accustomed trees, stepping without fail on the narrow paths between the irrigation channels of dry mud. The Prince ran round him, ran by him, crying and calling out and tugging at his loincloth, snatching at his hand. So the blind man hurried on, muttering and shaking his head and fending with his stick.

"Poor child! Poor child!"

At last, breathless, crying, and half-blinded by the sun, the Prince gave up, slackened his pace, trailed and came to a stop. He knelt down in the dust and wept for a time. When he had done weeping he stayed there, head down; and presently he began to recite phrases as if trying them for size or making sure he would remember them.

"I don't know what he's talking about. I can see quite well with both eyes."

And again; a phrase picked up perhaps in the corridors of the Great House.

"The man's possessed."

Again—simply.

"I am the Prince. The man's lying."

He got on all fours and stood up. He kept his eyes slitted and walked in the shade of trees. As he went, he repeated the words to himself like a lesson. "The man's lying. The man's lying."

Then there was a flurry of skirts, a shower of talk, a babble. The two nurses, the black one and the brown one, swooped on him and gathered him in. He was enveloped, enbosomed, cried over, cursed over, adjured, admonished, loved and smothered. They bore him off towards the Great House and after a while they put him down and hugged and kissed him, cleaned his skirt, caressed him in sweat and smell, in mammary abundance and fat arms. They told him how wicked he was to pretend to sleep while they slipped out to watch the God—told him how they had looked all over—how he must tell no one—how unkind he was to his nurses who had no single thought nor moment without concern for his happiness. Then they led him, hand in hand, to a side gate of the Great House, took him in and smartened him quickly for show. He may not have heard of the dangers from crocodiles, river monsters, lions, jackals or dirty old men; for he muttered to himself every now and then without paying attention to them.

"He's lying."

At last they led him through the Great House towards the courtyard that lay inside the main gate. Even though this was the day for the God to prove himself the courtyard was almost empty. But outside the main gate two rows of soldiers—black men with huge shields and spears—kept a lane clear, and the people of the river valley massed behind them on either side. The noise from them had sunk from the clamour that announced the beginning of the God's run. They had looked enough now, even at Pretty Flower where she stood in front of her women on a dais by the gate. They were tired of peering down the lane and along the path under the cliffs by which the God would return. The shawms were silent, Pretty Flower motionless if decorative, the God out of sight; and they needed something else to look at and the Prince provided it. He appeared at the inner edge of the forecourt, on the steps that led down from the entry to the Great House. He was flanked by fat, painted columns, and fat nurses. His pleated kilt had no dust on it and the gold studs of his sandals gleamed. So did the little necklace hung over his shoulders and the bracelets on his wrists. As for his sidelock, it had been combed, brushed, oiled till it looked like a shape cut out of ebony. He had a faint, public smile round his lips, and as the women in the crowd cried out how sweet and pretty he was, the smile became one of genuine pleasure. He paused by the dais, squinted up at Pretty Flower's face before its backing of fans, then lowered his hand to his knee in the appropriate gesture. His nurses helped him on to the dais and he stood there, blinking. Pretty Flower leaned, undulating. Her smile became one of love and she touched his cheek in an exquisitely feminine gesture with the back of her hand. She murmured down to him.

"You've been crying, you little runt."

The Prince examined his feet.

The noise of the crowd sharpened. The Prince glanced up and Pretty Flower took a step towards the edge of the dais, pulling him with her. From behind them, palm fronds were thrust into their hands. They looked where the crowd was looking, along the path.

Upriver, and just within sight, was a kind of foot of stone, sticking out of the cliff. There was a long, low building on this foot and a tiny figure moving by one end of it. Then a second figure appeared beside the first. They were difficult to see; and their movements were complicated by a wild vibration from the sunheat. They were manikins who changed shape with it or even disappeared in it for a moment. All of a sudden, the crowd on either side of the lane became thickets, hedges, groves of palm fronds moved by a perpetual wind. The shawms brayed.

"Life! Health! Strength!"

The first of the two figures was not the God. He was the Liar, the bony young man, who ran not only straight along the path, but back along it now and then, circled the God, made desperate gestures, urging him on. He sweated but was tireless, voluble. Behind him came the God, Great

House, Husband of the Royal Lady who had attained her eternal Now, Royal Bull, Falcon, Lord of the Upper Land. He was running slowly and sharpening his carving knife with a vigour that had a dawning desperation in it. He shone more wetly, and the kilt stuck to his thighs. He came out of the shuddering of the land and the sunblink. His white headgear had collapsed and he no longer jabbed at it with the crook or flail. Even his tail seemed affected and jerked about like the tail of a dying animal. He reeled sideways in his run. The Liar cried out.

"Oh, no!"

The crowd noises were as desperate as the runner's face.

"Great House! Great House!"

Even the soldiers were affected, turning sideways and breaking rank as if to help. The Prince saw a remembered figure with a stick edge between them into the path. The blind man stood there, face up, stick out. The God came thudding down the lane and the crowd closed in behind him. The blind man was shouting at the top of his voice—shouting something completely inaudible. The God's feet made an irregular pattern in the dust. His knees were bending, his mouth opened wider, his eyes stared blindly. He was falling. He struck the blind man's stick, his arms dropped, his knees gave. Still staring, he fell on the stick, rolled and lay still. The headgear of white linen trundled away.

In the sudden silence, the blind man was heard at last.

16

"The Prince is going blind, God! Your son is going blind!"

The Prince made a despairing gesture upward to Pretty Flower who was still smiling. He cried out his lesson.

"He's lying!"

"The Prince is going blind!"

Pretty Flower spoke clearly, calmly.

"Of course he's lying, dear child. Soldiers—take him to the pit."

The soldiers were pushing, striking out, clearing a space round the fallen God and the Liar who crouched by him. The crowd was swirling round the blind man who became a toy, a shouting doll. Pretty Flower spoke again.

"He tripped the God with his stick."

Other soldiers got at the blind man. They fought round the group on the ground; they got the Blind Man between them. Pretty Flower took the Prince by the wrist, shook it, and spoke sideways down to him.

"Smile."

"He's lying, I tell you!"

"Little fool. Smile."

The tears ran into the Prince's smile as she pulled him away from the dais, and then with what dignity was possible, through the Main Gate. Soldiers forced a way for them, and others carried the God. Pretty Flower and her women hurried the Prince to where the nurses took him and bore him and his tears out of sight. Then she and her women disappeared too.

17

A procession met the God in the forecourt as if it had been prepared for just this occasion. There was a couch borne by six men. There was a man in a leopard's skin and one—if he was a man—with the head of a jackal. They were led by a tall man much older than Great House, who wore a long robe of white linen. The sun winked from his shaven head. The Liar reached him first, still talking.

"Terrible, terrible, Head Man—and so unnecessary—that is, I mean—terrible! How could you have known? How could you guess?"

The Head Man smiled.

"It was a possibility."

"Remember I have no claim—no claim whatsoever!"

The Head Man smiled down at him benignly.

"Come now, my dear Liar. You undervalue yourself."

The Liar leapt as if a soldier had pricked him with a spear.

"Oh no, no! Believe me, I have no more to give!"

The God was on the couch. The procession moved towards the Great House. The Head Man watched it leave.

"He likes to hear your lies again and again."

The Liar stopped him before the entrance, holding him by the robe.

"He's heard them so often he could remember them himself—or get someone to make pictures of them!"

Turned half-back, the old man looked at him.

"That's not what He said yesterday."

"Indeed I assure you, I'm not in the least necessary!"

The old man turned right round, looked down, and laid a hand on the Liar's shoulder.

"Tell me, Liar—as a matter of interest—why do you avoid life?"

But the young man was not listening. He was peering past the old man into the Great House.

"He will, won't he?"

"Will what?"

"Run again! He was tripped. He will won't he?"

The old man examined him with a profound professional interest.

"I don't think so," he murmured gently. "In fact I'm sure he won't."

He walked to the Great House alone. The Liar stayed on the steps, jerking, trembling, and tugging at the pallor round his mouth.

Pretty Flower took most of it out on the Prince. In the comparative privacy of the Great House, she sent him off with a slap on the cheek that made up—as he had known it would—for all the affection on the dais. He went to bed whimpering, as the sun set.

The Liar was not disposed of so easily. He caught her alone in a dark corridor and seized her by the wrist.

"Unhand me!"

"I haven't handed you yet," he whispered. "Can't you think of anything else but sex?"

"After what you did——"

"I did? *We* did, you mean!"

"I won't think of it——"

"You'd better not. You'd better succeed. You'd better keep your mind on it!"

She slumped against him,

"I'm so tired—so confused—I wish—I don't know what I wish."

His arm crept round and patted her shoulder.

"There, there. There, there."

"You're trembling."

"Why shouldn't I tremble? I'm in deadly danger—I've been in it before; but never like this. So you'd better succeed. Understand?"

She stood away from him and drew herself up.

"You want me to be good? You?"

"Good? No—oh, yes! What you call good. Be very good!"

She moved past him, stately and pacing.

"Very well, then."

A whisper pursued her down the corridor and floated to her ear.

"For my sake!"

She shivered in the hot air and kept her eyes averted from the dim figures looming from the high walls. There was a noise now to hide any whispering—a confused sound, from the banqueting hall, of voices and music. She passed the hall to the farther end and drew aside a curtain. Here a space had been curtained off and lit with many lamps; and here her women waited, silent for fear of those henna'd palms and painted nails. But Pretty Flower had little thought for her women this evening. Silent and withdrawn, pure and determined, she allowed them to undress her, anoint her, spread her hair and change her jewels. She went and sat before her mirror as at an altar.

The mirror that Pretty Flower used was priceless. It was fabulous. For one thing, it did not reflect merely her face, but her body as far down as the waist. If she leaned still farther forward she could even see her feet. Only the Great House held treasures such as that. Then again, apart from the size of the mirror it was neither copper nor gold as was customary if a woman had a mirror at all. It was of solid silver which gave back to the user the most precious gift of all—a reflection with neither flattery nor distortion. The winged sky goddesses who held the mirror on either side were gold, and supported the shining centre in an impersonal way, as if determined to exert no influence on the user which might sway her judgment. The surface of the mirror had been rolled, beaten, ground, polished, until there was no other surface to which it might be likened. Indeed, as a surface it could not be said to exist, unless you breathed on it, or touched it with your finger to assure yourself of the invisible solidity. The surface was a concept, was nothing but a reversal that brought the world face to face, not with its own image, but with itself.

21

Absence of distortion, absence of flattery was exactly what Pretty Flower needed. She sat, gazing at her magical sister who gazed back, and they both became absorbed. The women in the brightly lit room recovered from their fear and began to murmur together as they busied themselves about her. She did not feel them nor hear them. She sat on a stool before the low table that supported the mirror. She was naked now, except for a belt of blue and gold that marked her waist without constricting it; and this last was just as well since any constriction of that slenderest part of her body would end what nature had so nearly completed and divide her in two. Flattery from the mirror or any other source would have been superfluous. Pretty Flower had achieved an exuberant Now; and no change could have been an improvement. They had heaped up her shining black hair out of the way on her head, though a curl or two had escaped. Her eyes did not blink for her absorption had deepened. The surgeon's stare before the body, the artist's before his work, or the philosopher's inward gaze at some metaphysical region of thought—none of these was more concentrated and abstracted than Pretty Flower's stare at her own image.

She was considering a colour evidently, for she held a bruised reed in her right hand where she could dip it with decision into the array before her on the slate palette. She could choose malachite crushed in oil, or crushed lapiz, or white or red clay, saffron. She could choose gold if she wanted to for on a small stand next to the palette hung little sheets of gold leaf that trembled like the wings of an insect in the heat from the naked lights.

"They are ready——"

But Pretty Flower ignored her women—indeed, was unaware of them. By some exercise of mental force, some inner pain, she had thrust herself up out of indecision to a level of clear understanding. Crimson it should be, must be, by the obscure but logical pressures of the rest. Her underlip slid out from where her upper teeth had gripped it against the lower and she nodded to her magical sister. Crimson enhanced with blue—not the dark blue of midnight, hardly to be distinguished from the black, nor the dense, grainless blue of midday over against the sun—but azure with white in it, seeming to shine from below the surface. With infinite care, she applied the colour.

"They are waiting——"

Pretty Flower laid the titstick among the others on the table.

"I'm ready too."

She dropped her arms and the bracelets tinkled as they fell to her wrists. She undulated to her feet, and the light shone, ran together, pulled out or disappeared over the dark brown smoothness of her skin. The women covered her, swathing her, wrapping her in folds of fine lawn; and she wound herself into them, moving more and more slowly, till the seventh veil covered her from hair to instep. Then she stood still, listening to the roar of conversation and sound of music from the banqueting halt She drew

23

herself up—unaware perhaps that she spoke aloud, in tones of sorrow and resolution.

"I will be good!"

Inside the banqueting hall the conversation had reached that point in a meal where it becomes a steady note. No one gave the Great House more than a casual glance every now and then. Since he seemed content to eat and drink and chat with the Head Man or the Liar, it was only courteous to ignore him—to pay him the courtier's supreme compliment of apparent indifference. For this reason, the long tables down either side of the hall contained groups which, while they were held together by the string of the occasion, nevertheless behaved as if the string was an elastic one. For if three guests—two women and one man, perhaps—seemed absorbed in themselves, even so, after only a few moments, one would be drawn into the next group which would divide correspondingly. All down either side of the hall, behind the tables and under the steady note, it looked as if the lillied head-dresses were stood in water and moved by a gentle wind. No courtier was drunk yet. Though their inspection was covert—as if by nature and not art—they had contrived to drink dish for dish with the God, no less and no more. Since he was older than anyone but the Head Man, and since he was evidently better at drinking than running, they would soon be drunk; they would soon be drunk, but not before the God was.

He was not as animated as his courtiers. He was recovered and content. He lay on a broad couch big enough

for two. Leather cushions were so heaped that his left elbow disappeared among them. Just now, he held what was
left of a roast duck in his right hand and ate delicately. The
Liar and the Head Man sat below the couch on either side
of the low table where the rest of the meal was. The Head
Man was quiet, smiling, and watching Great House with
an air of friendly attention. The Liar was as fidgety and
jerky as ever.

Great House finished the duck and held it out behind
him where it vanished in dusky hands. Other hands held
out a bowl into which he dipped two right fingers and a
thumb, twiddling them. As if this were a cue, the three
musicians squatting to one side at the other end of the hall
began to play more loudly. They were blind. Presently one
of them sang nasally, the old, old song.

> *"How sweet are thy embraces,*
> *Sweet as honey and hot as a summer night*
> *O my beloved, my sister!"*

The God peered glumly at the singer. He crooked his
little finger and took another dish of beer out of the air.
The Head Man raised his eyebrows, still smiling.

"Is that wise, Great House?"

"I want a drink."

All along the tables the dishes were being refilled.
Everyone felt thirsty.

The Head Man shook his head.

"It's a very long dance, you know, Great House."

The God belched. The roar sagged for a moment, then came back, punctuated by belches. Over the left and in a corner, one lady, with brilliant resource was noisily sick and everyone laughed at her.

The God tapped the Liar on the shoulder.

"Tell me some lies."

"I've told you all I know, Great House."

"All you can think of, you mean," said the Head Man. "They wouldn't be lies if you knew them."

The Liar looked at him, opened his mouth as if to argue, then slumped a little.

"Have it your own way."

"More lies," said Great House. "More lies, more lies!"

"I'm not very good at it, Great House."

"Tell me about the white men."

"You know about them."

"Go on," said the God, playfully tweaking the Liar's ear. "Tell me what their skin's like!"

"They look like a peeled onion," said the Liar dutifully. "Only not shiny. They're like that all over——"

"——every *inch* of them——"

"They don't wash——"

"Because if they did, the paint would come off!" Great House roared with laughter as he finished speaking and everyone else laughed too. The lady who had been sick fell off her chair, shrieking hysterically.

"And they smell," said the Liar, "like I told you they

26

smell. Their river runs round their land in a ring and rises up in great lumps and is salt, so that if you drink it you go mad and fall down."

Great House laughed again, then was silent.

"I wonder why I fell down," he said. "It was quite extraordinary. One step I was running, then the next step wasn't there."

The Liar jerked up.

"You were tripped, Great House—I saw it. And you drank all that beer before you ran. Next time——"

"You weren't drunk, Great House," said the Head Man, still smiling. "You were exhausted."

The God tweaked the Liar's ear again.

"Tell me about—" he laughed suddenly—"when the water goes hard."

"You heard it before."

The God thumped the couch with his right hand.

"Well, I want to hear it again," he said. "And again and again!"

The roar sagged and died away. The curtain at the end of the hall was drawn back on either side. Between them was a sort of monolith of white linen supported on two little feet. It advanced on them a span at a time until it stood in the centre of the space between the tables. The drummer began to beat very softly.

"—really as hard as stone," said the Liar. "In winter, the rocks by a waterfall are bearded with it like a pebble with weed. But it's all water."

"Go on," said Great House passionately. "Tell me how white and clear and cold it is, and how still—that's very important, the stillness!"

From somewhere, a black girl had appeared. She held one end of the outer shawl and gathered it in as the little feet turned beneath. The Liar continued to talk to the God; but his eyes flickered sideways.

"The marshes are black and white and hard. The reeds might be made of bone. And there is cold——"

"Ah! Go on——"

"Not just the coolness of evening or a breeze off the river. Not just the coolness of a porous water jug; but cold that seizes a man, makes him dance at first, then makes him slow, then brings him to a full stop."

"Did you hear that, Head Man?"

"If he lies down in the white dust which is water, he stays where he is. Presently he becomes stone. He is his own statue——"

Great House cried out.

"His Now is still! It moves no longer!"

He flung his arm across the Liar's shoulder.

"Dear Liar, you are very precious to me!"

The Liar was dirty white round the lips.

"Oh no, Great House! You are just being kind and courteous—I am of no importance to anyone!"

But the Head Man was coughing. They both turned towards him, and his eyes showed them where they were expected to look. The shawl was just slipping from the monolith. A shining torrent had fallen free. The head was turned away but began to nod on this side and that. The torrent glittered, swung in time to the drum. The feet worked and turned.

"Why," cried the God, "it's Pretty Flower!"

The Head Man was nodding and smiling.

"Your lovely Daughter."

Great House raised a hand in greeting. Smiling over her shoulder, Pretty Flower turned her back in exquisite time to the music and another shawl came off as the shining fall of hair swung femalely from hip to hip. Along the tables the roar had changed in quality to accord with the God's smile and wave. There were affectionate smiles everywhere, gentle cooings, a delighted welcome for Pretty Flower into the family. The reed instrument and the harp joined the drum.

"She's grown, you know," said Great House. "You wouldn't believe how much she's grown!"

The Liar tore his attention from Pretty Flower, licking his lips. He leaned towards Great House and came near to nudging him.

"That's better than hard water, eh, Great House?"

But the God's eyes had focused a long, long way beyond his daughter.

"Tell me some more."

The Liar frowned and thought. He came to some decision. He bent his bony face into a salacious grin.

"Customs?"

"Customs? What customs?"

The Liar whispered.

"Women."

He hunched himself still nearer and began to whisper behind his hand. The God's eyes became intent. He smiled. The two heads moved closer and closer together. The God reached behind him and brought another dish of beer to his mouth without looking at it. He sucked. The Liar began to shake with a prolonged snigger and his words came out from behind his hand.

"—sometimes they've never even seen them before— *strange* women!"

Great House snorted, and sprayed the Liar with beer.

"You can tell the most dirty——"

The Head Man coughed once more, with severe meaning. The rhythm of the music had changed. The reed instrument seemed more nasal, more plangent as if it had discovered something it wanted but did not know how to set about getting it. Pretty Flower had changed too. She was nakedly visible above the waist and she moved more quickly. Once, her feet had been all that moved. Now they, and her head, were all that was still. Her smile had gone, and she inspected her breasts, one at a time. For example: she would stand, right arm across her face, forearm down, palm outward and indicating her left breast, while her left curved to indicate it from below. Thus, her breast was delineated by two palms, offered, as it were, and made to pulse and quiver gently by a subtle rotation, of the left

30

shoulder so that its warmth and weight and scent and tex-
ture was evident. Then bonelessly, she would evolve into a
mirror image, this time concentrating on her right breast.
It was now, with a brace of crimson nipples shaking out a
perfume into the heavy air, that the reed instrument began
to understand what it wanted. The nasal tone became a
more than human cry. This cry was taken up along the
tables, where there was some kissing among the drinking
and a little delicate pawing. The Liar's head turned slowly,
compelled from Great House. His mouth was pinched as if
with thirst.

"She's beautiful," he groaned. "Beautiful, beautiful!"

"She is indeed," said the God. "Tell me some more,
Liar."

The Liar groaned in agony.

"You must watch her, Great House—don't you understand?"

"There's plenty of time for that."

Pretty Flower was doing things with both breasts. Her
hair flashed and floated wildly. The Liar was torn between
her and the God. He beat his head with both hands.

"Very well," said Great House sulkily. "If you won't tell
me any more I shall play checkers with the Head Man."

The board appeared at once, like the beer. As Great
House leant over it and shook the dicing sticks in the cup,
a change came over the tables. There was less pawing,
more muted conversation about food and drink and social
matters and games. Pretty Flower and the musicians

31

seemed to be performing to themselves, or the air.

"Your move," said Great House. "Good luck."

"I've sometimes thought," said the Head Man, "it might be interesting if we didn't let chance decide the moves but thought them out for ourselves."

"What an odd game," said Great House. "It wouldn't have any rules at all."

He glanced up, saw Pretty Flower and gave her a quite charming smile before he looked down again. She was indicating the smallness of her waist and the complex bearings of her hips which were moving in a slow circle beneath the last shawl. If there was any expression to be read behind her elaborate make-up it was one of anxiety, turning to sheer desperation. As she went into each new figure of the dance, she prolonged it, as if to enforce the invitation by sheer strength. She gleamed with more than unguents.

This was hard on the musicians. The harpist raked at the strings with the insistence of a woman rubbing out meal between two stones. The reed player's eyes were crossed. Only the drummer beat easily, changing hands now and then, using two sometimes, sometimes only one. Along the tables, the talk was of checkers or hunting.

"Your move, Head Man."

The Head Man shook his head and the dicing sticks at the same time. The Liar, greatly daring, was tugging at the God's skirt for attention. The last shawl had come off Pretty Flower. She was naked and shining except for her jewels. Her mouth, drawn down at the corners in a stylized grimace of desire, had set round her gleaming teeth. She went into her last figure. This began at the other end of the hall, and brought her—the music commanding it and giving it power—in a series of convulsions down the whole length. Every few yards it threw her into display, arms out, knees apart, belly thrust forward. It brought her down the hall from a Now to a Now to a Now. Her thighs struck the God who struck the checker board and the ivory pieces flew in every direction. The God jerked back angrily and stared up.

"Do you *mind*?"

Then there was silence along the tables, silence from the collapsed musicians, silence from the dais where the ivory pieces had ceased to roll, and the only things that moved were the breasts of Pretty Flower. She fell, collapsed on the floor of the hall, face downward.

Great House moved, the anger dying out of his face. He passed the back of his hand across his forehead.

"Oh yes. Of course. I forgot."

He swung his legs off the couch and sat on the edge.

"You know, I——"

"Yes, Great House?"

Great House looked down at his daughter.

"Very good, my dear. Most exciting."

The Head Man leaned close.

"Well then——"

The Liar was hopping and desperate, between Pretty Flower and the couch.

33

"You must, Great House! You must!"

Great House had either hand laid on the couch beside him. He braced his hands, stiffening the muscles of his arms. He drew himself up, drew his stomach in, so that some faint indication of a muscled torso appeared beneath the quivering thickness. He stayed so for a few moments.

"Great House—please! Dear Great House!"

The God let out his breath. His eyes unfocused. His body slumped between slackened arms and his insides bulged out slowly into a smooth and rounded belly. He spoke flatly.

"I couldn't."

The sound of indrawn breath was like the flyby hiss of a monstrous arrow. Not a face in the hall but stared down. Not a finger or an eye but was motionless.

Suddenly Pretty Flower scrambled to her feet. She hid her face in her hands and fled shuddering and stumbling down the length of the hall and the curtains swung together behind her.

A young man came hurrying from the shadows at the back of the dais. He bent and whispered in the God's ear.

"Oh yes. I'll come now."

The God got to his feet and the hall rustled as everyone else got to their feet too; but all faces still stared down, all mouths were silent. Great House followed the young man through the shadows and out into the open. Over the courtyard night was growing heavy at the zenith, oozing down and uncovering a myriad skypeople as it came.

Beneath the creeping night and nearer to the horizon the sky was lighter blue, fragile, hardly able to bear the impending weight. Great House paused only to glance round at the fragility, whistled softly, then hurried to one of the four corners. He muttered to the young men as he went.

"I've cut it fine tonight, haven't I?"

In the corner was a low altar built against the wall. Great House cleaned himself with holy water as he gazed round him apprehensively at the darkening sky. He dropped a pinch of incense on the glowing charcoal, then muttered a few words so that a thick column of white smoke pushed up into the darkness. He went hurriedly to the other three corners and made more columns. He stood for a while checking on the columns; then turned away to go back to the banqueting hall. As he went he muttered again, either to himself or the young man.

"At least I can still keep the sky up."

In the hall, the guests were ranged behind the tables, looking down, and saying nothing. The Liar knelt by the couch, his hands fastened to one of the legs as if it would save him from drowning. Great House heaved himself on to the couch and lay on his side.

He spoke.

"I should like a drink."

But before anyone could move, the Head Man had caught him by the wrist and was speaking to him through his quiet smile.

"Don't you understand, Great House?"

Great House turned to him. His solid face quivered.

"Understand?"

"This morning you fell. This evening——"

Great House caught his breath. Then he began to laugh.

"You mean, it's a beginning?"

"Just so."

The silence behind the tables broke up. There was a sudden gust of whispers.

"A beginning! A beginning!"

The Liar let go the leg of the couch, grabbed at the curved head, knelt there, eyes shut, head up. He shouted.

"No! No!"

But Great House still laughed. He swung his legs off the couch and sat there, laughing and speaking directly to the assembly.

"Strong beer and no hangover!"

The Head Man smiled and nodded.

"Beautiful, changeless women——"

The Liar began to babble at the God.

"Of course, Great House! What else does any man need? Beer and women, women and beer, a weapon or two—what else does anyone need?"

"His potter," said the Head Man. "His musicians. His baker, his brewer, his jeweller——"

Great House tweaked the Liar's ear.

"And his Liar."

The Liar's babble ran up so that all other sound in the hall died away. The Head Man patted him.

"Calm yourself, my dear Liar!"

The God looked down at him, his smile broadening. He was in high good humour.

"What's all this? I simply couldn't do without you!"

The Liar screamed once. He leapt to his feet, glaring round him. Then he was off, sprinting down the hall. He dived over the musicians and took one of the curtains with him. There was a scuffle and a series of thumps, soldier-sounds, blows. There were orders. The Liar yelled again.

"I won't!"

The scuffles and thumps receded down the corridor; and once more, but fainter this time, the assembly heard the Liar, shouting in terror and indignation.

"You fools! Can't you use models?"

Nobody moved. Every face in the hall was flushed with shame. The darkness where the curtain had been torn down was like an obscene wound in the fabric of life itself.

At last the Head Man broke the silence.

"No more tiredness."

Great House nodded.

"And I shall make our river rise. I swear it."

Now, along the tables, people began to laugh and weep.

"Forgive your Liar, Great House," murmured the Head Man. "He is sick. But you shall have him."

The guests were beginning to move towards Great House from the tables. They wept and laughed and stretched out their hands. Great House dashed a tear from his eye.

37

"Dear family! My children!"

The Head Man cried out.

"Bring Great House the key!"

The guests moved into two groups that left a passage down the hall. Presently, from the darkness beyond the place where the curtain had been, a little, old woman came veiled and slow and carrying a dish. She gave it to the God, then turned aside into the shadows. Great House received the drink and laughed with excitement. He held the dish up with both hands. He cried out in a loud voice.

"To keep Now still!"

He drank and drank, tilting back his head; and softly, with tiny shuffling steps and a muted clapping of hands the guests began to dance. As they danced, they began to sing, nodding and looking at each other with shining eyes.

> *"The river is filled to the brim.*
> *The blue flower lies open;*
> *Now moves no longer."*

Great House lay back on the couch and closed his eyes. The Head Man leaned over him moving his limbs, setting his knees together, smoothing down the rumpled kilt. The musicians began to play, catching the time from the dancers. The dance quickened and the God smiled in his sleep. The Head Man took his arms and folded them across each other so that they lacked nothing but the crook and flail. He tried the pulse in the left wrist, listened, ear against chest, for breathing. He stood up, moved to the end of the couch and slid the pillow from beneath the sleeper's head.

"The river has risen and will not fall" they sang. *"Now is forever!"*

They were moving in a complex weave that sorted itself little by little into concentric circles. The lamps flickered in the wafts of hot air. Servants and soldiers filled the spaces of the doors. Kilts and transparent dresses stuck to flying limbs.

The Head Man stood behind the couch and faced the dancers. He lifted his hands. The dance stilled, the music fell silent, instrument by instrument. He beckoned and soldiers and clean men pushed through the crowd. They formed round the couch, then lifted it easily. They bore it through the hall and away into the deeper and darker mysteries of the Great House. Then the guests went silently, not looking back. The banqueting hall was empty of all but the Head Man. He stayed where he was, looking at the lamps and smiling faintly. Presently, he too went away to sleep.

Only one part of the Great House remained awake. This was an upper terrace that fronted the distant river; and here, a group of women crouched, saying nothing, but staring in silence at the girl who lay sprawled in her hair with nothing but one snatched-up shawl to cover her naked body. There was tension in her every limb. The forearm on which her smeared face lay, ended in a frenetically clenched fist that jerked every now and then at a sob. Sometimes the other hand would crawl over the floor then beat on it, and from her squarely opened mouth, a long wail would issue like a child crying. When the cry had ended, she would sniff and hiccup and moan words in-to the silent air.

"Oh the shame, the burning shame of it!"

When the river rose at the behest of the Sleeper, the only living things taken unawares by the expected were those most immediately connected with it. The cranes and flamingoes would stagger, flap and squawk when the minute rising built up into an occasional ripple. After the first one, they greeted the rest with bird noises of satisfaction. They became busy and zestful at the unexpected ease of life. They pecked and gulped as if they were hard put to it to keep pace with the fertility of the dried mud which once wetted, spawned all kinds of agreeably edible life. When only a few inches of water were thrusting across the stubble, the ducks came in flotillas, quacking complacently and allowing themselves to be carried by the push of the flood. The hawks and buzzards that were normally indifferent to the fields now hung in a line over the limit of the advancing water. The shrews and fieldmice, the snakes and slow-worms that had no built-in foreknowledge of the inundation and now made a panic way towards higher ground, learnt a bitter and useless lesson. But the people who knew why the river was rising and knew what full bellies it would bring were filled with joy and love for the

Sleeper, so that when the air was cool enough they sang and danced. In the hot time, since there was nothing else to do, they sat in the shade and watched the waters advance. When dusk released them from the tyranny of the sun, they would walk, splashing through an inch or two of warm water over mud as hard and rough to the feet as a brick, and perhaps bend and lave themselves. Those who went deeper to the limit of their fields to catch a view they remembered, felt the first slipperiness of the slime and stood, rubbing their feet in it with a pleased smile.

When the water had reached the Notch Of Excellent Eating—when the hamlets had been so long isolated that some of the younger children thought it a Now that never moved—the day of waking slid into place. It dawned like every other day, green, then red, then gold, then blue. But the people heard the shawms braying and looked at each other laughing, since the shawms and the Notch Of Excellent Eating had come together.

"Today the Sleeper wakes into his Now and will send the waters back."

For this reason they kept watch from the roofs of their houses and explained the thing to their children. All morning the shawms brayed and the drums beat; and then at midday when the sun glared down at the flood which steamed back at him they saw the procession set out along the strip of dry land left between the cliff and the flooded earth. They saw how the Sleeper himself lay at the head of the procession. He lay on a litter carried by eight tall men.

41

He was swaddled from head to foot and richly plumped with his hands crossed over his chest and the crook and flail in them. He was of many colours but mostly gold and blue; and even at a distance they could see how his beard jutted against the shivering of the cliffs. The long-haired women came dancing after him, crying out, some trying to wake him, each with a systrum in her hand, others wailing and cutting themselves with knives. After them came clean men and other people of his household; and then a group of men and women who walked sideways, hand in hand. It was a slow journey the Sleeper took. It was a long and slow procession that straggled behind him, or paced frieze-like on the causeways by the water. Many of the villagers, drawn by love and curiosity, climbed down from their roofs and waded towards the procession. They stood, big-eyed as children in the water and watched it pass. They called out to the Sleeper, but he did not wake since the clean men still had work to do on him. So they stood, since wading, they could not keep up with even such a slow mover and they greeted the groups one after the other.

There was one group they did not greet but watched in silent disbelief. At the tail end of the procession and separated from it by a gap, came a detail of soldiers with the Liar struggling among them. The collar of Great House was round his neck as were his collars round the necks of those who walked sideways and hand in hand. If the Liar—as he sometimes did—contrived to get a hand free, he would tear at the collar with it. Moreover, sometimes he shouted, and sometimes he screamed, and sometimes he moaned; but all the time he struggled with the soldiers so that they had a hard job not to spoil him. He was in a fair way to spoil himself for there was a scum of foam round his mouth. His noise penetrated most of the way up the procession.

"I won't, I tell you! I don't want to live! I won't!"

The last man of the handholders looked back then turned again to the woman in front of him.

"I could never understand what Great House sees in him."

The waders climbed on to the causeway and hurried after the procession and the Liar. When the land broadened and the procession stopped, breaking into separate groups, the waders became a crowd.

The procession was grouped before that long, low building round which Great House and the Liar had run. There was a passage, now, that led down before them, between sloping sides of rubble and the farther end was in deep shadow, away from the sun. The opening into the building occupied only half the width of this passage; and to one side of the opening, there was a slot, at eyelevel. Those in the procession who were near the beginning of the passage, could see the slot; and even those too far off, or hindered from seeing by the crowd, knew the slot was there, and what would gaze out of it.

The bearers took the Sleeper down the passage, lifted him off his couch and stood him on his feet but facing out into the air. The people, crowding forward, could see that he was still asleep, for his eyes were closed. But the clean men came with their instruments and powerful words; so that presently his eyes opened, and a clean man threw away the clay that had kept them closed. So the Sleeper woke, and Great House stood and stared through his family out of his motionless Now, in life and health and strength. Then the Head Man—since he was a clean man among other things—performed his office. He wrapped the life of a leopard round him, girding it at the waist. He lifted a small adze, with a flint blade, and he forced the blade into the wooden mouth. He levered with it, and those who were near enough heard a crackle like fire among small branches. When the Head Man stepped back again, the people could see that Great House was speaking a word in the motionless Now, for his mouth was open. So the dancing and singing began. But among the dancing and singing, many people wept a little to think how elusive their own Now was, and no more to be caught than a shadow. The soldiers, the bearers, and the clean men took Great House out of the passage and on to the roof of the building where the rare and heavy logs had been laid aside so that there was a gap. They took Great House down with them; and the soldiers who stood on the roof round the hole, saw the God laid in a stone box, saw the lid slid into place and sealed. Then the clean men climbed back and left the God among his chambers of food and drink and weapons and games.

They stood and watched, while the soldiers put back the logs and levered the huge stones over them.

As the clean men had done with Great House, so they did with his Twin who stood erect in darkness behind the slot. Only when the Head Man came with the adze, he did not lever the mouth open because it was stone but touched it merely. As for the eyes of the Twin, they were already open, and stared out of the slot.

Then those who had linked hands crowded forward and were given each what they had to carry. They went forward between the rows of clean men, the stonecutter with his drill, the carpenter with his adze and chisel, the baker with his yeast, the brewer with his malt, the women finely dressed and painted, the musicians with their instruments under their arms. They laughed and chattered as they came in, and they received their bowls of drink with pride and delight. Only the Liar still struggled; and now his screams had an even more piercing point to them. The Head Man tried to soothe him, calling him sick and be-witched but the Liar would not listen.

"If you do, I'll never tell him another lie—*never*!"

At that, the dancing faltered, and the favoured ones in the passage looked back in shocked surprise. The Head Man slapped the Liar sharply on the face so that for a moment he fell silent with the shock, sniffing and twitching.

"Calm yourself, Liar. Calm yourself. Now. Tell us. Why do you refuse eternal life?"

It was then that the Liar said the awful thing, the dirty

45

thing, the thing that broke up the world. He paused for a moment. He ceased to sniff. He gave a convulsive wrench of his whole body that staggered the soldiers who held him. He crouched among them, glared back at the Head Man in fury and shouted the words at the top of his voice.

"Because this one is good enough!"

The words silenced every sound except the quick panting of the Liar. The dancing stopped and the Liar was surrounded by a ring of shocked and contemptuous faces. Suddenly, as if he felt this contempt was thrusting him towards the God, he began to struggle fiercely. The Head Man held up his hand. The Liar stopped struggling and stared at this hand as if his life was held in it. The Head Man spoke quietly, like a physician explaining a disease.

"Great House never found a man who refused a favour from Him. But this man is unclean and must be cleaned. Take him to the pit."

The Liar stayed tense only until he felt the soldiers turn away. Then he fell and would have collapsed in the sand if his arms had not held him to the soldiers like ropes. The soldiers walked away, dragging the Liar with them and his head lolled and his mouth stayed open. The crowd watched, saying nothing. The soldiers dragged the Liar back along the causeway and out of sight.

Then the people, as if united more than ever by this extravagant event, turned back to the passage. Those who waited in the passage with their instruments and bowls of drink, began to sing, and move forward; and those who disappeared at the farther end, when they could no longer be seen, could no longer be heard either, so that the singing diminished as the visible numbers decreased. When there were only two left, the song was hardly loud enough to be heard outside the passage. Then there was one, then none, and only the faintest suggestion of sound that lingered round the passage end. The crowd listened, straining, leaning forward, heads on one side—not knowing whether there was indeed a faint sound or only the memory of it. At last there was undoubted silence; and sorrow rose among those who were left with their private Nows to cope with. This sorrow was gradual as the diminution of the singing but undoubted as the silence. It came up out of the earth. The women began to wail and beat their breasts and tear their hair; and the men moaned like trapped animals. Only the clean men were untouched by this sorrow. They took food and drink and fire. They closed the entrance with powerful words, offered food and drink at the slot and spoke to the unwinking eyes that stared back at them out of the darkness. They came up out of the passage and walked with the Head Man back along the causeway. The crowd walked, drifted, waded away. Only the soldiers were left. They began to work, filling the passage with stones and sand.

The Prince was being made to practise the godpose. The Head Man had taken him away from his nurses and sat him in a suitable chair. There he was, in the gloomy banqueting hall, knees and feet together, chest out, chin lifted, eyes open and staring at nothing. He wore a child-size ceremonial outfit, complete with tail; he held the crook and flail crossed before his chest. They had taken away his lovely side-lock and he was bald as a pebble beneath the close-fitting wig. The tall, linen crown was fastened to his wig, and a beard was strapped to his chin. He sat, trying to breathe imperceptibly and not blink, while the gloom wavered and the tears of effort formed in his eyes.

The Head Man strolled round and round him. The only noise came from the faint swish of his skirt.

"Good," said the Head Man. "Very good."

Round and round. One of the tears rolled from the Prince's clouded eye down his cheek. He gave up, and blinked furiously.

"There," said the Head Man. "You were doing so well but you spoilt it. Keep them open and the tears will come for the people. Don't blink!"

"I must blink! People blink!"

"You will not be 'People'," said the Head Man crossly. "You will be the God, Great House, throned in state, holding power in one hand and care in the other."

"They'll see me cry!"

"They are meant to see you cry. It is a profound religious truth. Do you suppose any God who keeps his eyes open can do other than weep for what he sees?"

"Anyone would weep," said the Prince sullenly, "if he

kept his eyes open and didn't blink or rub them."

"'Anyone'," said the Head Man, "would blink or rub them. That's the difference."

The Prince straightened himself and stared again into the gloom. He saw the wide rectangle of the entrance at the other end of the hall lighten, and knew that the sunlight was creeping along the corridor towards it. He gave up, shut his eyes and bowed his head. The crook and flail clattered in his lap. The Head Man stopped strolling.

"Not again!"

"I can't do it. Keeping the sky up—bouncing up and down on my sister—keeping my eyes open—making the river rise——"

The Head Man struck one fist into the other hand. For a moment it seemed as if he would burst out in fury; but he mastered himself, bowing his head, swallowing, breathing deeply.

"Look, child. You don't know our danger. You don't know how little time there is—your sister withdrawn—seeing no one—the river rising——"

He bent down and peered into the Prince's face.

"You *must* do it! Everything will be all right. I promise. Now. Try again."

Once more the Prince took up the godpose. The Head Man watched him for a while.

"That's better! Now. I have to see your sister—have to! So I shall leave you here. Stay as you are until the sun reaches from one side of the entrance to the other."

He drew himself up, raised one hand, lowered it to his knee, took three steps backward, then turned and hurried away.

When the swish, swish of the Head Man's skirt was out of earshot, the Prince let out all his breath and slumped, eyes shut. He raised a bony forearm and smeared it across his face. He shifted his skinny rump, where the tail was making it ache. He laid the crook and flail on the floor by the chair. He looked at the doorway for a moment; then tore the linen crown from his head, so that the close-fitting wig came with it, and the narrow strap of the beard broke. He flung the whole thing down on the crook and flail. He hunched, glumly, chin on fists, elbows on knees. A grain of sunlight on tiles flashed into view and he screwed up his eyes against it. The grain enlarged to a brilliant patch.

He jerked upright in the chair, then began to walk restlessly, pad, pad, round the huge room. He glanced now and then at the walls, where the bird-headed, dog-headed figures did not weep. He stopped at last, in the middle of the room with his back to the sunlight. Slowly he lifted his head, peered up at the gloomy beams and awful solidity of the rafters. He flinched away from the sight as if the beams threatened to fall on his head.

He went softly to the entrance and looked into the corridor. At one end, a guard leaned against the wall. The Prince squared his shoulders as best he could and walked steadily towards the guard, who woke and lifted his spear.

The Prince ignored him and turned the corner, where a girl backed submissively against the wall to let him pass. He went away through the Great House, ignoring all the people he met until he came to the back and heard the muted noises from the kitchens. He passed them, the cooks lying asleep, the scouring and staring scullions, their court where geese roasted slowly over charcoal on spits under the open sky. The postern gate to the cliffs and desert was open. He took a deep breath, like a boy about to dive, clenched his fists, and passed through.

Outside the gate, he paused in the shadow of the wall and examined the knees of cliffs, sandscrees, the line of rock-edge against the sky. Everything was fierce and barren. There was nothing as pleasant as palmshade by water; but there were plenty of places to hide. He began to make his way forward and up, keeping where he could in the shadow of rocks, though there was little enough of that. As he went, he muttered.

"*She* can keep it up!"

He was crying.

He stumbled sideways and crouched behind a boulder, peering round it. There was a man among the rocks. This man knelt on a knoll of rock so that he was outlined in profile against the cliffs. His head was bowed as though the sun had struck him down.

The man knelt up. He began to do something regular with his arms and suddenly the Prince understood that the man was pulling a string or a rope out of the earth.

51

No sooner had he understood this than he saw some bowls and platters appear under the man's hand—held perhaps in a net of cords too thin to be visible. The man stood up, made a jeering noise and spat down at his feet. He took up a stone and threatened the ground with it. He pretended to throw down once or twice, then did throw strongly and a scream came up out of the rock. The man turned and came strolling back, laughing, and swinging the string bag with its bowls and platters. The Prince shrank down behind his boulder and listened as the man went back. He was trembling, and went on trembling long after the postern gate slammed shut.

He got up, shading his eyes with both hands and went forward. The sun fell on his bald head and beat back from the rock. He limited himself to his one good eye and climbed the knoll.

The first thing he was aware of was the smell; then after, the flies. The knoll swarmed with them. Their buzzing increased with every step he took, and soon they discovered him.

He found himself on the edge of a pit. The sunlight lit it right to the bottom, except on one side, where there was a little shade by the wall. The flies liked the pit, evidently, for they buzzed away down there and covered the refuse, the bones and decaying meat, the slimy vegetables and stained stones. The blind man lay in one corner under the sun, his head propped against rock. The only difference between his bones and the others was that his were still covered with skin. He was very dirty. His mouth was open and his tongue showed where the flies did not cover it. As the Prince realized who he was, he heard him make a tiny sound, without moving either his lips or his tongue.

"Kek."

Near the centre of the pit and in a small area cleared of refuse, knelt a man. The Prince inspected him, then cried out.

"Liar!"

But the Liar said nothing and went on drinking. His head was in the bowl between his hands and he sucked busily, louder than the blind man's kek, or the flies buzzing. He lifted his head and the bowl together, to take the last drop. His eyes were above the bowl's rim. He glimpsed someone kneeling on the edge of the pit and ducked away.

"Don't!"

"Dear Liar! It's I!"

Cautiously, forearm lifted for protection, the Liar squinted up. His face was blistered and dirty except where there was new blood on it, and his eyes were rimmed as red as the blood.

"The Prince?"

"Help me!"

The Liar stumbled round in the refuse. He yelled back.

"You? You don't need any help! What about me?"

"I've run away."

"I'm dreaming. I'm seeing things. They said I was mad—and now——"

"I don't want to go back."

The Liar put both fists above his eyes and squinted upward.

"It's really you?"

"They're turning me into a god."

The Liar spoke with dreadful urgency.

"Get me out of here! That sister of yours—tell her to help!"

"She won't see anyone," said the Prince. "And besides, I'm running away. We could go together."

The Liar went still.

"You? Run away?"

"We could go and live where it's cold."

"Oh so easily," said the Liar, jeering. "You just don't know!"

"I've got as far as this by myself."

The Liar gave a kind of yelling laugh.

"We'd go down the river, across the sea, across the land, then more sea——"

"Yes, let's!"

"Have you ever been swopped for a boatload of onions?"

"No, of course not."

"Or felt up by a Syrian to see if you're too old to make a eunuch?"

"What's a Syrian?"

"We'd be sold again as slaves——"

The Liar paused, licked his cracked lips, stared slowly round the pit then up again at the Prince.

"Half a boatload, perhaps, only you're not very strong and you're not very pretty, are you?"

"I'm a boy. If I were a girl I'd be pretty. And not have to make the river rise, or——"

"Those bracelets you're wearing," said the Liar slowly. "They'd be thrown in. You might make a eunuch."

"I'd sooner be a girl," said the Prince with a touch of bashfulness. "Could it be arranged, do you think?"

Under the dirt, there was a still look of calculation on the Liar's face.

"Oh yes. Get me out of here and——"

"Then we're going? Really going?"

"We're going. Now listen——"

"Kek."

"Why does he make that noise?"

"He's dying," said the Liar. "Taking a long time."

"How did he break his stick?"

"I tried to climb out of the pit with it, but it broke. I was standing on his shoulders and he fell down."

"I think he's thirsty."

"Of course he is," said the Liar impatiently. "That's why he's dying."

"Why didn't he have any water?"

"Because I needed it," shouted the Liar. "Have you any more silly questions? We're wasting time!"

"All the same——"

"Listen. Did anyone see you come here?"

"No."

"Could you bribe people?"

"The Head Man would find out. He knows everything."

"You're too small to carry a ladder. But you could bring a rope. You could tie it round a rock and let the end down——"

The Prince jumped to his feet and clapped his hands.

"Oh yes, yes!"

"That sister of yours—*she* wouldn't have a rope—of all the ignorant, thick-headed, maddening, beautiful—Could *you* find a rope?"

The Prince would have danced in his happiness and excitement, had he not been so near the edge of the pit.

"I'll find one," he cried. "I'll look!"

"And another thing. You've more jewels than you're wearing."

"Of course."

"Bring them."

"Yes, yes!"

"A rope. Jewels. After dark. You swear?"

"I swear! Dear Liar!"

"Go on, then. It's my—it's our only chance."

The Prince turned away from the pit and was a few yards down the rock, before he remembered and crouched sideways under cover. But the guard was not lounging by the postern gate. There was nobody in sight at all; and the gate was shut. He decided to pick his way towards the shade of the palms and the flooded fields, then wade through the few inches of water round the side of the Great House to the main gate. But at the edge of the fields he found two naked boys playing with a reed skiff. He told them to take him to the main gate and they did so at once, not speaking, in awe of his bracelets and necklace, his sandals, his Holy Tail and pleated skirt. So he walked through the forecourt and went straight to his rooms; he woke his nurses out of their siesta, and because he was so nearly a god, they found it easy to obey him in his new determination. Jewels he must have, many jewels; and when they dared to ask why, he looked at them and they went. Finally he had the jewels heaped before him; and it was a strangely pleasant task to hang them on himself, till he clattered and tinkled as he moved.

The rope was another matter. The Great House seemed short on available rope. There were ropes at the wells by the kitchens but they were too long and too hard to get at. There were rope falls and guys to each of the masts that stood, their pennants hanging limp before the main gate. The Prince became a little vague and sat tinkling in a corner to consider what he should do. In the end he saw one thing clearly. He could not find a rope. Those servants he asked, bowed, sidled off and did not come back. He heaved a deep sigh, and began to tremble. If you really needed a rope, there was only one man to ask for it—the man who knew everything. Slowly, and tinkling, he got to his feet.

The terrace was raised, and the balcony fronted on the swollen river. An awning was spread over it, and the fabric hung dead in the motionless air. Pretty Flower was in the shade of the awning. She sat, staring at the water. She was changed, and reduced. Her long hair had been cut across the forehead and right round lower down so that it did not quite reach her shoulders. Though her head was bound with a fillet of gold from which rose a cobra's head in gold and topaz, she was thinner in figure and face, and the only make-up she wore was the heavy malachite that lay on her eyelids and matted her eyelashes into necessary shade. So she stared sullenly at the water; and if her expression was to be read, it was as one of shame, brazened out.

The Head Man stood before her. He held his chin in his right hand and rested his right elbow in the palm of his left. He was smiling still, but his smile was tight.

Pretty Flower lowered her chin and stared at the pavement.

"You see—I failed. I know He's angry with me. All the time I know it."

"With me too. With all of us."

"I shall never, never forgive myself."

The Head Man stirred. His smile became wry.

"We may none of us have the time."

She looked up, startled. Her bosom went in and out.

"You mean he'll drown us all?"

"There is a—strong possibility. That is why I have ventured to thrust myself on you. I said there is little time. None the less, we who are responsible for the people must do what can be done. We must take thought. You see,

Pretty Flower—in this emergency I may call you Pretty Flower, may I not?"

"Anything."

"What distinguishes man from the rest of creation?"

"I don't know!"

"His capacity to look at facts—and draw from them a conclusion."

He began to pace to and fro on the terrace, hands clasped behind his back.

"First," he said, "we must establish the facts."

"What facts?"

"Who kept the sky up? Mm?"

"Well—He did."

"Who, year after year in His—paternal generosity—made the river rise?"

"He did, of course."

"*This* time—is there another God yet?"

"No," said Pretty Flower heavily. "Not yet."

"*Therefore*—who makes the river rise now?"

"He does. I thought——"

The Head Man held up one finger.

"Step by step. Yes. He does. We have established the first fact. Now for the second. How high was the water when He entered His Motionless Now?"

"At the Notch Of Excellent Eating."

"Which was after the occasion when you say you failed. But at that time He must have been pleased. You see?"

"But——"

"Your woman's heart must not struggle against the granite durability of rational demonstration."

Her eyes widened.

"What does that mean?"

The Head Man meditated for a moment.

"The words are difficult admittedly; but they mean that I am right and you are wrong."

She straightened in the seat and smiled a little.

"Partly, perhaps."

"Nevertheless, do not be too happy, Pretty Flower—not too happy!"

"There is no fear of that."

"The fact, then. Something angered Him after he entered the House of Life."

He paused, and resumed his pacing. Then, at the point of a turn, he stopped and faced her.

"They have said—and it would be false modesty to deny it—that all knowledge is my province. What a man can know, I know."

She looked back at him under her heavy fringe of lashes. A smile moved only one corner of her mouth.

"You know about me, too?"

"I know that you have been in this deep seclusion. Now these things have to be said, otherwise we cannot deal with them. His anger concerns a person in whom—unconsciously perhaps—you take a deep interest. There. I have said it."

For a moment her face was dusky with blood; but the

smile stayed where it was.

"Again, I don't know what you mean."

"I refer, of course, to the Liar."

The blush came and went but her eyes never left him. He continued in the same cool voice.

"It is necessary, Pretty Flower. We cannot afford the comfort of self-deceit. There is nothing you cannot tell me."

Suddenly she buried her face in her hands.

"Wrong upon wrong. Vice so ingrained, wickedness so deep, so dirty——"

"Poor child, poor, poor child!"

"Monstrous thoughts and indescribable——"

He was close to her. He spoke gently.

"Leave these thoughts where they are and they fester. Take them out and—they are gone. Come, my dear. Let us be two humble souls, hand-in-hand, exploring the tragic depths of the human condition."

She slumped to her knees before him, face in hands.

"When he sat at, at the God's feet and told Him—told us—of the white mountains floating in water—how cold he was—a white fire; and he so poorly dressed, so helpless and so brave——"

"And you wanted to warm him."

She nodded miserably, without speaking.

"And little by little—you wanted to make love with him."

His voice was so detached that the strangeness, the

impossibility of their conversation was taken away. He spoke again, mildly.

"How did you justify yourself to yourself?"

"I pretended to myself that he was my brother."

"Knowing all the time that he was—a stranger, as in his fantasies of white men."

Her voice came, muffled through her palms.

"My brother by the God is only eleven years old. And the fact that the Liar was—what you said—*can* I tell you?"

"Be brave."

"It put a keener edge on my love."

"Poor child! Poor twisted soul!"

"What will happen to me? What *can* happen to me? I have shattered the laws of nature."

"At least, you are being honest."

She moved towards his knees and put out her hands to embrace them, face up.

"But then—when we *did* make love——"

There were no knees to embrace. They were a yard away, having removed themselves with the speed of a man avoiding a snake. The Head Man his hands clenched against his chest was staring at her past his shoulder.

"You—you and he—you—the——"

She sat back on her knees, arms wide. She stared at him and cried out.

"But you said you knew everything!"

He went quickly to the parapet and looked at nothing. For a while he said absurd, childish things.

62

"Well. Oh dear. Well, well, well. Tut, tut. Bless me!"

At last he stopped muttering, turned and came towards her—yet not directly towards her. He cleared his throat.

"And all this, this—stood between you and your lawful desire for your father."

She said nothing. He spoke again, his voice raised and indignant.

"Can you wonder that the river's still rising?"

But Pretty Flower was standing up. Her voice rose like the Head Man's.

"What do you want? You're supposed to be doing your practice!"

The Head Man followed her eyes.

"Have you been listening, Prince?"

"You've been spying," cried Pretty Flower. "You nasty little boy! What have you got all those things on for?"

"I like them," said the Prince, trembling and tinkling. "I didn't hear anything much. Only what he said about the river rising."

"Oh go away!"

"I won't stay," said, the Prince quickly. "I was only wondering, as a matter of fact actually, if either of you had a piece of rope——"

"Rope? What for?"

"I just wanted it."

"You've been outside the gate again. Look at your sandals!"

"I just thought——"

63

"Go away and tell those women to clean you."

The Prince, still trembling, turned to go; but the Head Man spoke with sudden authority.

"Wait!"

Bowing slightly to Pretty Flower, as if asking for permission he went to the Prince and took him by the arm.

"Be pleased to squat down, Prince. Here. Excellent. We want rope and we've been outside. You were attached to him, weren't you? I begin to understand. And the jewels—of course!"

"I just wanted——"

Pretty Flower was looking from one to the other.

"What *is* all this?"

The Head Man turned to her.

"This touches directly on our conversation. There is—but you would not know precisely where—a pit. When you say 'Take him to the pit——'"

"I know," said Pretty Flower impatiently. "What has it to do with me?"

"Some of the terrible causes of our danger cannot be undone. But one at least, can. The God is angry with His Liar and makes the waters rise, in part, because the Liar refused the gift of eternal life."

Pretty Flower jerked half out of her chair. Her hands were clenched on the arms of it.

"The pit——"

He bowed his head.

"His Liar still endures the vexations, the insecurities,

the trials of a moving Now."

He caught her just in time, lowered her gently to the chair and began to slap her hands. He muttered to himself again.

"Oh dear, oh dear, oh dear!"

The Prince found his voice.

"Can I go now?"

But the Head Man paid no attention to him. The Prince listened in silence as the Head Man gave orders to soldiers at the door, watched without comment though perhaps a little envy as Pretty Flower's beauty was put back on her face by her women. A tiny old woman brought in a bowl of drink and placed it on a pedestal by the chair. Then the three of them waited and the sun lowered towards evening.

Pretty Flower cleared her throat.

"What will you do?"

"Persuade him. Let me administer such consolation to you as I can; for you must be strong. You think yourself exceptional. And of course you are—exceptionally beautiful for one thing. But these dark desires—" he glanced for a moment at the Prince, then away—"you are not alone in them. In all of us there is a deep, unspoken, a morbid desire to make love with a, a—you understand what I mean. Not related to you by blood. An outlander with his own fantasies. Don't you see what these fantasies are? They are a desperate attempt to get rid of his own corrupt desires, to act them out in imagination; because—by the laws of nature—they cannot be externalized. Do you suppose, my dear, there are real places where people marry across the natural borders of consanguinity? Besides, where would they live, the puppets in these fantastic lies? Suppose for a moment the sky to be so big it stretched out to cover these lands! Well—think of the weight!"

"Yes. Madness."

"You admit the truth to yourself at last. A madman whose lies have—for all of us—stirred up the central, unspeakable plenum; a madman who is a peril to us all unless he agrees to serve the God."

He paused, turned away to look at the flooded valley. An empty boat came twisting and turning down the central current.

"You see? We cannot afford to wait for a cure. If he cannot be persuaded—we will try, of course—then we must use force."

There was silence for a time. Pretty Flower began to cry again. She did not interrupt the silence with her crying. The water swam down her cheeks and the malachite came with it, like spill from a mine. The river continued to rise. The Prince sat, tinkling every now and then.

Presently Pretty Flower stopped crying.

"I must look a mess."

"No, no, my dear. A little—disarranged, perhaps. Becomingly."

She signalled for her women.

"You know, Head Man? It shows how far I have been

corrupted. I very nearly don't care. Not quite, of course but very nearly."

He looked down at her, frowning, puzzled.

"About the flood?"

"Oh *that*—no. My face, I mean."

The women went away again. Pretty Flower settled herself firmly.

"I'm ready now."

The Head Man spoke loudly.

"Have him brought here."

The Prince scrambled to his feet.

"Well—I think—I'll go and have a drink———"

The words came hissing from the chair.

"Stay where you are, you runt!"

The Prince sat down again.

There were noises beyond the terrace and among them the sound of a well-known voice talking, voluble as ever but at a higher pitch. Two tall black soldiers wearing nothing but loincloths dragged the Liar forward between them. The soldiers brought him round and held him before Pretty Flower. He stopped talking and looked at her. She looked back at him with eyes like stones and would have seemed secure as a dweller in the house of life, if it had not been for the way her dress shivered over her breast. The Liar caught sight of the Prince, squatting beyond her by the wall. He convulsed between the soldiers and yelled at the top of his voice.

"*You*—traitor!"

"I didn't——"

"Just one moment, Liar." The Head Man turned to Pretty Flower. "Shall I?"

She opened her lips, but no sound came out. The Head Man lifted a finger.

"Let him go."

The two soldiers backed away from the Liar, glistening. They unslung their spears and held them pointed at him as if he were a beast in a net. He began to talk again, quickly, desperately, from person to person.

"Poison is cruel. You may say it doesn't hurt but how do you know? Come now, have you ever been poisoned? I have many secrets that would be of use to you. I could even stop the river rising—but I must have time, time! We don't any of us like being frightened, do we? It's horrible to be frightened—horrible, horrible!"

The Head Man interrupted him.

"We aren't frightening you, Liar!"

"Then why, when I stop speaking, do my teeth sing in my head?"

The Head Man put out his hand to the Liar who flinched away.

"Calm yourself, my dear man. Nothing is going to happen to you. Not at this moment."

"Nothing?"

"Nothing. Let there be a pause. Relax, Liar. Just lie down and curl up comfortably on the mat."

The Liar looked suspiciously at him; but the Head Man

only nodded and smiled. The Liar put out one hand to the floor, knelt, looking up sideways. He glanced round him, winced at the sight of the spears, then slowly laid himself down. He pulled himself into a parody of the foetal position; but no foetus was ever so tense, so quivering. No foetus ever stared so, up, sideways, and round.

The Head Man glanced at the swollen river and winced from it as the Liar had winced from the spears. Visibly he pulled himself together.

"Now, Liar. There's nothing to be frightened of. We have all the time in the world."

He saw an unblinking eye, looking up warily as a crab under a rock.

"Close your eyes. Let everything go."

The eye closed, snapped open, then shut once more but left a gleaming slit. The Head Man spoke softly.

"Let us think of real things."

The Liar jerked and quivered on the floor.

"Death. Murder. Lust. The pit."

"No! No! Gentle things, soft things, homely things!"

The gleam shivered, expanded, then disappeared. The foetus murmured against the floor.

"Wind on the cheeks. Coolth."

"Good."

"White flakes tumbling. Mountains that wear a white cloak——"

"There you go again! Real things, I said!"

"White men. Pure, white women, ivory and

69

gold—strangers all—and thus available. Oh the kindness of a strange woman by a strange hearth!"

The Head Man was so strung up that he sniggered then glanced at Pretty Flower apologetically. Her dress was shivering again.

"Listen Liar. Now you are calm, I am going to make one last appeal to your generosity. You are dear to the God. It angers Him that you will not go to Him. Accept the gift of eternal life—for our sake!"

The Liar yelled.

"No!"

"Wait. We understand you are sick and ungenerous. Therefore to help you help us, we will be generous too. We will give you as much as we gave Him."

"Bribery?"

But the Head Man was not listening. He had begun to pace round and round the Liar, whose head followed his movements like the head of a snake.

"Mind, even that may not be enough. After what I have heard recently, He may be so angry that—but we must do what we can. Do you suppose we ask you to join the others in the periphery and lie there merely heat-dried? Oh no, indeed! We will take off the stones and the beams——"

"What are you talking about?"

"You shall lie by the God Himself. In no less than three coffins, the innermost to be made of such materials—however rich—as you shall specify."

The Liar was kneeling. He yelled again.

"You old fool!"

"Wait till I finish. We will cut you open and clean you out. We will pull your brains through your nostrils and fill your skull with liquid fragrance——"

And carried away, the Head Man was making ample gestures round his own body. The Liar had wrapped his arms round himself and was hooting like a demented owl.

"——we will cut off your public parts——"

The Prince leapt to his feet.

"Oh yes, yes!"

The Liar stopped hooting and began to speak, more and more violently.

"A patch of land no bigger than a farm—a handful of apes left high and dry by the tide of men—too ignorant, too complacent, too dimwitted to believe the world is more than ten miles of river——"

"You'll drown us all!"

"Drown then, if you haven't the wit to climb the cliffs away from it——"

"We implore you!"

"Myself, trapped, condemned, the only sensible man in this, this——"

He flung himself forward and grabbed Pretty Flower by the foot.

"Don't you understand? Your brother is—what is he—ten? *You* have the power—the power, the power, the power! Do you want to marry him? That miserable shrimp of a boy——"

"Unhand me!"

"He'd sooner be a girl. You have the soldiers—you, one of a dozen petty chieftains that line this river—you have the beginnings of an army——"

Pretty Flower was gasping for breath. Her hands were up by her face. She stared at him as if his eyes were the only place to look. The Liar spoke again.

"Do you want to marry him?"

Her mouth opened and shut. Her hands on the arms of the chair drew back. Her knuckles whitened. She took her eyes from his face, glanced at the smiling Prince, at the bowl on the pedestal.

"You have the beginnings of an army. What could you not do?"

The Head Man spoke.

"We know what to do."

But as if he had found some hope, some security in Pretty Flower, or even some power over her, the Liar stood before her and spoke like a God.

"The man who holds the high seat in this country is the man who has you, strange and beautiful woman, for his bed. He could burn up the banks of this river from one end to the other, until all men living by it were bowing to your beauty."

"Who on *earth*," said the Head Man, "would want to do a thing like that? I said you are mad!"

"I am not mad. There is no deceit and no wickedness in me."

Pretty Flower cried out.

"No wickedness? After what you said about strange women?"

The Liar flung his arms wide.

"Don't you see? You've none of you seen! In this land of halfwits there is only one man with access to all women —Great House, the God!"

Pretty Flower was standing up, her hands over her cheeks. But the Liar had turned and was staring at the Head Man in hatred and contempt.

"Not even you—a man thought wise—all this nonsense of my not having that woman, that girl, that beautiful—and her wanting me——"

He stabbed out a finger in the Head Man's face.

"Supposing I were Great House?"

Under his dark skin, the Head Man's blood ebbed away then came rushing back. He took three steps away from the Liar.

"Soldiers—kill him!"

The soldiers moved forward behind their spears. The dignity dropped from the Liar like a fallen cloak. As if fear and hate had possessed him like a God, he did instant and impossible things. His body took charge of his face. He swerved sideways and forward, turned. The soldiers passed him and even before they had stopped this movement, one was tripped and falling and his spear had whipped into the Liar's hands. Nor could eye follow the snake-tongue of the point as it snicked in and out of the soldier's neck. The other soldier turned but only in time to meet the point. He flapped at his chest and fell in a disjointed way. He had not reached the floor before the Liar had faced round to the Head Man, who shouted at the top of his voice.

"Bowmen!"

The Liar's spear made magic passes round the Head Man who did nothing. Talking, the Liar sprinted across the terrace and leapt to the top of the parapet. He turned back, just as the bowmen came running with their unstrung bows. He threw the spear, and a bowman fell, his string still coiled in his hand. All the time, as his body did these impossible things, the Liar talked and talked out of his worried face. Even when he leapt from the parapet he talked. He dived neatly into the flood water and perhaps he talked under there as well; only when he surfaced, labouring great armfuls of water out of the way, there was too much noise on the terrace for anyone to know whether he talked or not. Arrows were digging into the water round him, then floating away, feathers upward.

The Head Man was changing. He was holding his midriff and looking at once far away and inside himself. He lowered himself on one knee. There was a collapsed look about his face. It was smaller, older.

The Prince had changed too. He ignored the dead and dying. His smile was bright, as he spoke to Pretty Flower, though she paid him no attention.

"Then my eyes wouldn't matter, and I wouldn't have to be a God, would I?"

The Head Man spoke with his cheek against the floor.

"Bleeding inside. He stings like a scorpion."

Far away and beyond reach of anything but random shot, the Liar had climbed out of the water to the top of a wall that, like a narrow path, led onward beneath the heads of palms to the central current of the flood. He turned back to the terrace, arms gesticulating, miming silently, but staunchlessly, the mechanics, the necessity of survival. The bowmen stood by the parapet, their quivers empty. They were turning to Pretty Flower for orders; but she still stared after the Liar, hands up, mouth open.

The Head Man made his last statement, clearly, professionally.

"He has a death wish."

The Prince's grin was so wide it was ridiculous.

"Can I have a drink now?"

She answered him absently.

"Presently, dear child."

She moved forward towards the parapet.

"A death wish. All the same——"

The bowmen waited, looking at her. She was changing too. She was becoming rounder, plumper, even. The gloss included her eyes, her hair. Those planes that had been her cheeks were now curved. As if some perfume concealed in her body was taking aromatic and excited charge, she shone, she sparkled. There was colour beneath the curved

75

cheeks, where the beginnings of a smile revealed their dimples. Her arms were up, their henna'd palms outward, gesture reserved for revelation.

"All the same—we'd better go and talk to Him."

CLONK CLONK

Song before speech
Verse before prose
Flute before blowpipe
Lyre before bow

I

Palm listened to the Bee Women, her smile like applause
so that they were happy as she intended. There was
no disease, and yes, the bees were bringing back honey
from the plain as well as from the forest. You could
taste the plain in the honey, a spice, an aroma. Yes. The
bees were doing well. When she had used her smile as
much as was necessary she turned away to take it back
the short distance to the space between the river and
the straw huts, the lean-tos and shelters in the tumbled
rocks. It was the space the children played in, hot and
dusty now, but not as hot as it would be, when the sun
was at height. The children felt the heat, she saw that at
once; for two small boys were fighting in more than play
and only fell apart when they saw her and her smile.
Another boy—smaller this one and not much more than
a baby—came toddling with an egg in either hand and
held them up.

"Clever," she said, "Clever!"

She tousled his hair and walked on. It was time the
children went for their midday sleep. More of them were
making a fuss, by the bank of the river, three boys and two
girls. The girls were marching along by the boys in step.

They raised sticks together in their right hands. They chanted.

"Rah! Rah! Rah!"

One of the boys was red and crying, already. The other two had their heads bent down and were making marks in the dust. The two girls turned, lifted their sticks, saw her and took them down again, giggling. They looked away, rubbing one foot over the other. She spoke quietly to them as she passed.

"Play somewhere else, will you?"

There was plenty of space and plenty of children—boys throwing things or wrestling, girls playing with dolls, skipping, or talking together. Palm let each group have a share in her smile as she passed. She set herself to climb.

The morning sun had removed the mushroom top from the vapour over the Hot Springs. There was little more than a faint mist over the highest point of the rise, where the boiling water seethed up. Lower down, in the string of pans where the water cooled to lukewarm and lost itself in the river there was no vapour at all. Still, once you climbed the littlest way from the place where the children played the air was fresher as if it had moved down from the mountain rather than in across the plain. She decided there and then that she would bathe just one pan higher than usual. She looked forward to the long soak for she felt the faintest creak in one shoulder and hoped that the hot water would take it out. She climbed, then, with dignity, and with a grace hardly modified at all by the creak.

Her long grass skirt rustled, her naked toes gripped and relaxed on the worn rock. Still, she admitted to herself that her heart beat more heavily than it was used to. She stopped halfway up, flicked the water of a pan as if to see how hot it was—or as if to remove a dead leaf or insect. She straightened up, turned round and inspected what lay below her, pretending it was her custom to do so from here rather than later on, at the summit, by the boiling spring.

The women were working in the woods and in the Place of Women. She could not see them but she could hear their chatter and occasional high laughter. Where the woods thinned out and the water from the hot springs met the river, young girls were wading waist-deep and hauling a net. She could see how the diminishing area of water was stippled as if with raindrops and knew they had caught a shoal. Beyond that again, the Bee Women were working among the straw skeps. Much food, girls working and laughing, many children, two women suckling babies among the rocks, another heavily with child and even now, being helped by her sisters to a shelter, Hot Springs, warm air——

She spoke to herself as she did now, more and more often.

"There is too much food. Not meat perhaps, but fish, eggs, roots, honey, leaves and buds——"

She put both hands on her belly above the grass skirt. Her smile was rueful.

"And I eat too much of it."

Well, she thought, I am getting older. That explains everything. I must not expect to be beautiful for ever.

She began to climb again among the pans, following the worn path through the white and green encrustations. The air warmed as she went upwards from pan to pan. The noise of the women and children diminished and at last was swallowed up in the seethe, plop, bubble of the boiling spring at the top. A girl stood there, on the little space of level rock by the spring. She was slim and her grass skirt was shortened to her knee. Her long, black hair was wound tightly on little sticks. She had a broad, uncomely face, but the grace of adolescence shone over it. She stood up straight when she saw who approached her. She laughed, and pointed sideways over the plain.

"It was there. In line with the cleft."

"You're sure, child? There are such things as grass fires, you know."

"It was a camp fire—Palm."

The girl hesitated at the name, still abashed at addressing her as one adult to another. But Palm had turned and was staring out over the plain. She pursed her lips.

"Then they'll work along that side of the plain, near the hills—where the dry ravine is. You'll see tonight's camp fire *there*—I should think. Unless of course they've changed their minds, or been frightened, or started fighting or something."

The girl giggled.

"Or something!"

Palm smiled at her.

"So they'll be away for two whole days. You can take your hair out of curlers."

The girl's mouth opened. She looked blank.

"Two days?"

"It might be more." She peered closely at the girl. "Angry Elephant, isn't he?"

"Oh no—Palm. He *was* Angry Elephant but now he's Furious Lion."

"Before he was Angry Elephant, he was Busy Bee, I think. Of course he was much younger then. You would hardly remember."

The girl's face had changed colour. She gave a wriggle and a giggle.

"You know how they are—Palm!"

"I do indeed. None better. Well—remember!"

The girl's face went solemn, and proud.

"Now I am a woman."

Palm made a gesture of assent and turned to go.

"Palm——"

"What is it?"

"The old Leopard Man——"

"Which one, child? We have three here, after all."

The girl pointed down.

"That one there."

Palm looked down, saw the bald head among the rocks,

the knobs of shoulders, the thin legs splayed out. The girl spoke at her shoulder.

"I don't know his names. But he hasn't moved for—oh for ever so long! And his breathing—I think he belongs to us now. He's a baby again. Isn't that right?"

"You did very well to notice. I will have it seen to. So. Keep good watch!"

She turned away and walked down; not the way she had come, but another, towards the bald head of the Leopard Man where she could see it below her. He was not far from the Lodge Of The Leopard Men. Poor thing, she thought to herself, he has got as close to it as he could! The rock was steeper above him, and she went carefully, frowning with the effort. But there was no frown on her face when she came to where he lay, his back against the rock, his legs stretched in front of him. His hands played restlessly with the scrap of worn and soiled leopard skin he held in his lap. His mouth was open and dribbling. His breathing was quick. She knelt by him and put a hand on his forehead. She peered into his eyes, where there was nothing. She smiled with infinite sweetness and murmured to the empty face.

"Sleep?"

She stood up quickly, crossed to the mouth of a shelter, and spoke into it.

"That man, that poor old thing—what is his name? Fierce Eel? Oh, yes, I remember—and Flame and Wasp. He needs you. Now, this moment."

She stood up and made her way across to the string of pans. Businesslike, she put the thought of the old man out of her mind. She felt pleasure in this high point of the day, good thoughts and feelings came crowding in. That nice child up there on lookout, she's so sweet, so eager—hot water—then when I've had my bath—we have at least two clear days—I'll see that it's plentiful, and good and strong——

She spoke aloud and ruefully again.

"I drink too much."

That was when she remembered what the Bee Women, the children, the lookout and the Leopard Man had pushed into a corner of her mind. The unease. It swelled out and filled her mind so that she made her sweet smile stay where it was. She thought: *I smile sweetly, as a cat eats grass for distemper!*

So she stood, dallying with the bath lest it should disappoint her and not soothe away the unease. She stared up the rise of pans through the faint mist over the boiling water at the top, to the mountain beyond, that had its own vapour. It rose hugely, jets of steam vented here and there from smears of red or yellow on black. Smoke rose from the top amid a crown of snow. At once she was aware of how the mountain looked down at her. She put both hands to her mouth, but stared back; because you always stare back when you are not only Palm but also She Who Names The Women; and then the mountain was just a mountain, and her unease was with her.

"I am still young enough to have a child. Perhaps when they get back——"

She glanced quickly this way and that but there was no male near—not even some ancient Leopard Man able to do no more than lie in the sun—not even some man child who might remember he heard what She Who Names The Women had said. There was no one at all within hearing. She dropped her hands and climbed upward to her bath.

The pans were each a little higher than the next, perhaps by the length of a forearm. Each brimmed and let a film of water seep perpetually over the smooth surround into the next. Sometimes the film was thicker than usual, as if the earth had changes of mood; but always the pans were full. This fulness was a source of pleasure to Palm, who felt it as a rich thing, a foison, a generosity of water. She was grateful to the water, without personifying it. The bath invited her. She put her hands to her waist and loosed the grass skirt so that it fell round her feet. She thrust her hands under her hair to the nape of her neck. But when she laid the rows of clattering shells on the rock, she did not climb immediately and step down into the soothing heat. She knelt, pushed back her long hair and peered into a cooler pan. She let the sunlight fall on her face, held her breath and stared at the face that swam up from the darkness.

"I am beautiful."

A tress fell and ripples made the face shake. She swept the hair back and stared down again. The dark eyes were huge, black patches, the face oval and neat. She put up a hand and felt its softness—felt too, though she could not see them, the beginnings of wrinkles by the mouth, the wrinkles of the neck where the shells had hidden them.

"I am still beautiful. That—cannot be it."

From the forest and Place of Women came the chatter and laughter of the girls. The children were silent, sleeping in the shade. She Who Names The Women stood up briskly. She climbed three pans higher and tried the top one with a toe. She stepped in, biting her lower lip. She sank into the hot water and sweat burst out of her skin. She squatted, willing herself to wait until her skin accepted the pain and became accustomed to it. At last she relaxed, lay back and rested her head on the stone that had been put there for the purpose. Her hair spread; and slowly her body rose, pale brown and green in the clear water. She floated, all but her head that rested on the stone. Her graceful body was laid out at the surface like a diagram of womanhood. She shut her eyes. There was a gap with no time in it.

From the shelter the woman hooted like an owl. Palm opened her eyes and thoughts formed immediately. Soon I shall have a baby to examine. A girl, I should think, from the way she was carrying. I hope—I hope whichever it is, we can keep it. I do not like——

The unease was back, wide, deep, ungraspable as water. She sat up, smearing back her hair. She twisted and stared up through the vapour to where the white head and dark shoulders of the mountain loomed under its own smoke.

Sometimes, she thought, the mountain looks up at the sky as if we weren't here; and sometimes the mountain stares down—as if we weren't here!

She shook herself so that the water splashed.

"A mountain is a mountain! Palm, you think like a man!"

So briskly she ducked her head, tossed it so that the hot water streamed from her face and hair. She began to massage her face with her fingers, busied herself with her own body, but all the time her thoughts busied themselves in her mind. Nothing is wrong. You can be happy or sad, you can be nothing in particular when you are thinking of what is to be done. But you cannot be uneasy at what *is*.

All the same, we are *menaced*.

She stood up, stepped down into cooler water, ducked, then got out and sat down to let the sun dry her. She bowed her head and began to run her fingers through her hair again and again. Feelings are feelings; but each hair must lie smoothly by the next. Presently attend to the dressing of it, the greasing of the face, the shaping of nails with an appropriate stone.

"Palm! Palm!"

It was the child from the lookout, swaying and leaping down between the pans, her hands up for balance, grass skirt flying.

"Palm! Oh Palm!"

Now she has learnt to call me that, thought Palm, she will use it every other word! She laughed at the child and blew her a kiss.

"Palm! Palm! Palm! I'm not a forest, you know!"

"I've seen them!"

"They're not coming back, surely? Not so soon?"

"Oh no! You were right, Palm. Palm—they're going farther. Ever so far! I wouldn't have been able to see them, but—" she giggled. "They're climbing a tree!"

Palm laughed back.

"All of them? For nuts? Or for a dare?"

"I could only see one—very high up."

"Bird's eggs."

"I thought you'd better know, Palm."

Palm put back her hair with one hand and patted the girl's cheek with the other.

"You did quite right—" She made herself remember—"Minnow. After all, that's what you're there for, isn't it? Now, help me with my skirt!"

"I wonder if it was Furious Lion? I couldn't tell of course, at that distance. What *fun* he must be having!"

She Who Names The Women was fastening her shells.

"It's pleasant to think of them enjoying themselves. I only hope they haven't forgotten what they went out for! Well. I'll come up with you and have a look. Lead the way."

Again the woman in labour hooted like an owl. Not too long now, thought Palm. I hope——

Minnow stood by the boiling spring, one hand shading her eyes. Her breathing had not changed.

"There. See the big tree, Palm, with the one bare branch

89

at the top? Well, just where it comes out of the leaves—can't you see him?"

"No, I can't," said Palm. "But if they've gone as far as that, they'll be bound for a long trip. You need not watch any more. Just come up here at sunset and spot their camp fire."

Minnow turned and looked shyly at her.

"What would happen if they—well. If they found out?"

"They won't."

Palm looked down at the Lodge of the Leopard Men. It was open to the sky and so open to examination from the high point by the boiling water. The rows of leopard skulls gleamed in the sun. She smiled and the smile turned into a long peal of laughter. Minnow began to laugh too. They were sisters, and of the same age while the laugh lasted.

Palm fell silent first.

"We shall do nothing, of course, until the child is born. And even then, only if the child is—is named."

Minnow went solemn.

"I understand."

Palm smiled, loving her solemnity. She leant forward and kissed her lightly on the lips so that the girl flushed and swayed back and caught her breath. Then Palm turned and began her way down, her breathing easy at the descent, her body swaying gracefully, hands out on either side. The walls of the Lodge of the Leopard Men rose up and hid the gleaming skulls. This time, she thought, I shall be careful! I shall drink hardly anything at all! But at that, as if her thoughts had pulled the thing out of the air, the image of a coconut shell full of dark liquid hung before her, vivid in every detail. She could even smell the stuff, so that she flushed and caught her breath as Minnow had done. It is in me, she thought, I am not like the others. I was born with it; and no Namer Of Women could look into me and see this, this——

The ancient Leopard Man no longer lay sprawled against the rocks. The children slept. Palm stood in the open space where the children had been, graceful and gracious; and smiling sweetly.

II

At the top of the naked bough that thrust up from the big tree, there was a nest of sticks. Bits of food hung in the sticks—skin, fur. A handful of red feathers fluttered at the edge. The Leopard Man who was shinning up the naked bough was hardly more covered than the bough itself except that he wore a narrow strip of hide round his waist and a close bag of it between his legs. The other Leopard Men stood round the tree in groups, looking upward over the crown of leaves and laughing. Each time Forest Fire slipped back down the bough at immediate risk to his neck, they shouted with a laughter that was total. They held on to each other, went wet-eyed and weak-knee'd. But when he tried again, this time more slowly and carefully and seemed to ooze up with a snakelike movement they fell silent and motionless, looking up. They stood elegantly, their spears with their fire-hardened points cradled in the crook of an arm. Some of the Leopard Men were not much more than boys, but most were slim young men of light brown, or seemed to be. There was little to tell their age. The elders among them could only be recognized by the streaks of grey in their hair. If they carried more weapons, more ornaments, more miscellaneous objects than Forest Fire oozing up his bough, nevertheless, they were substantially as naked as he—keen-faced men, unlined but scarred, with dark eyes and eyebrows and hair and dusty, naked feet. Their beards were no more than dark smudges on lip and chin.

Forest Fire was just under the nest. He took both hands from the bough, gripping it with his thighs and shins and insteps, and leaned backwards in the air, reaching out for the red feathers. The Leopard Men changed position in one lissom movement, miming attention and excitement.

"Ah——!"

Forest Fire grabbed the red feathers and thrust them into his belt. The Leopard Men opened their mouths to cheer—but instead, a scream came searing down the sky with talons and huge beak and a whirl of wings and feathers. Instantly there was a flurry of brown limbs and feathers at the top of the bough under the nest, there were feathers flying and blood. Then there was silence. Forest Fire, his face contorted, was twisting strongly with both hands. The bright blood slithered over him. He was a place of red snakes. He shouted aloud, and hurled the dead thing down into the crown of the tree. The Leopard Men laughed and slapped their thighs and hurried to the tree bole. Forest Fire slid down, clambered and shouted. Twigs, leaves and lichen came down before him. He swung, then dropped the last ten feet and was enveloped by his peers. The youths and elders stood round in a circle beaming with pleasure. The young men embraced and kissed him, careless of the blood or sharing it. There was laughter and chatter. Forest Fire broke away and chattered most of all.

"A scarlet feather for Furious Lion!"

"For me? Dear friend!"

"A scarlet feather for Rutting Rhino!"

"Best of men!"

"A scarlet feather for Stooping Eagle!"

"Sweetheart!"

Forest Fire was jerked under his blood, with effort and excitement. As they patted and kissed him, or thumped him on the back, he fell silent, feeling at his belt, then looking at his empty hands. His cheeks uncreased round his mouth which stayed open. He stared down to where his weapons and ornaments lay on the bare earth under the tree. He gritted his teeth. He snatched up his spear and hurled it at the bole.

"No scarlet feather for Forest Fire!"

He burst into tears.

At once, the other young men closed round him, singing and talking soothingly. Forest Fire sniffed and gulped. Furious Lion put an arm round his neck and kissed him and pressed the red feather into his hand.

"Look, Forest Fire, here is a scarlet feather for you!"

"No, no! I don't want it!"

"And here is another red feather for you——"

"And another——"

"I wanted you to have them. When I saw them, I said there are feathers for Furious Lion, and Rutting Rhino and Stooping Eagle——"

"Forest Fire hangs the scarlet berries round his throat——"

"Forest Fire hangs the scarlet berries round his ankles——"

"Scarlet feathers for Forest Fire!"

"I couldn't. Not now. Oh, do you really think so?"

"Bend your head down a little——"

"You're sure? You're not doing it just because I was so silly and weepy?"

"All three of them, straight up in front, I think. There!"

Forest Fire shook, and laughed through his tears. He bent down, put red berries round his neck, fastened, on anklets of red berries. Stooping Eagle took the instrument with three strings from where it hung over his shoulder and began to strum.

"Forest Fire burned up a tree from the root to the top!
Forest Fire plucked red feathers from the sun!"

Forest Fire leapt into the air. He began to run, leap, swoop, fly round the bare earth beneath the big tree. His arms were out and made wing movements.

"Look at me! I can fly!"

"And I can fly!"

"And I!"

Forest Fire stood, bouncing up and down, arms out.

"Look at me! I'm a beautiful bird!"

"He's a beautiful bird!"

"I'm a beautiful bird! See me! Hear me! Love me! I'm a beautiful bird!"

He swooped and flew to the Elder of Elders.

"Beautiful Bird?"

The Elder of Elders looked round with a stern face. He lifted his spear. There was much stately lifting of spears. There was silence. The Elder of Elders looked down. Forest Fire knelt. The Elder of Elders lowered his spear till it lay on Forest Fire's shoulder.

"Beautiful Bird."

Beautiful Bird stood up beaming, he shed a happy tear, he laughed. Stooping Eagle put an arm round his shoulder and kissed him.

In the silence there was a faint chattering. The Leopard Men swung as one, staring into the tall grass of the plain. The chattering came close, the grass moved, the chimps were coming back to the shade of their tree. The young ones broke into view and screamed. The mothers with young huddled back into the grass. The young chimps jumped up and down and showed their teeth. The Leopard Men stood sideways, leaning back on a foot. They stared in profile, chins up. The Boss Chimp rose, head and shoulders out of the grass. He bared his teeth and snarled. The Leopard Men laughed and jeered and made throwing motions with their spears. The Boss Chimp jumped up and down, snarling and beating the earth with his paws. The youths imitated him, laughing. Only the elders stood still, spears gracefully cradled, lips bent in a tolerant smile. The Boss Chimp stopped jumping up and down. He stood up on his hind feet, slowly and clumsily. He turned clumsily. Slowly and clumsily he laboured away, upright through the long grass. Only when it rose to his shoulders did he drop on all fours and lollop after his charges, out of sight.

When the chimps had gone the Leopard Men relaxed, singing and laughing. The Elder of Elders examined the sun-shadow he stood on which was not much longer than his foot. He stretched and yawned a huge yawn. The other men began to yawn too and move towards the bole of the big tree. They talked all at once but paid little heed to what anyone else said.

It was not speech that Palm or Minnow would have bothered to understand. They would have recognized, being women, that it was not useful speech. It was no more than an expression of an emotional state, so that in that sense, each Leopard Man was talking or singing to himself. Mime of the body, song of the throat, it was a communication at once total and imprecise as the minds that lay behind it. It conveyed contempt of the chimps, pleasure in the thought of sleep and love—love as unselfconscious as the sleep. One laid down his three-stringed bow, one his hand drum. They put off weapons so that there was a scattered jumble before the splayed roots. They snuggled, old and young together into the natural rest places between the roots so that the trunk seemed to grow a frill of brown skin and sliding muscles. The dappled shade shifted over them. The singing became a crooning, murmuring sound as they hugged and cuddled and made love. There was much stroking and intimate sharing till heat and satisfaction sunk them towards sleep.

But not all slept. There was a young man who had not crept into the mass of skin and togetherness. Nor, if it comes to that, had he avoided it. There were rest places on the other side of the tree but he had not gone to them. He sat instead, at the edge of the sleepers, where their feet reached. His knees were up to his chin and he glanced sideways, every now and then, without speaking. All the time, his hand caressed his ankle. There was a thick callous of skin on the bone, and a long bruise on the side of his foot under it. Sometimes he stroked the bruise, sometimes he picked at the callous; and his eyes looked from one face to another as the hunters made love or sank openmouthed and snoring, towards sleep. Once, the young man put his smudgy beard and moustache down on his knees and shut his eyes; but he soon lifted them again and stole glances sideways at the others.

Beautiful Bird was snuggled against a youth who lay in the crook of his arm. Beautiful Bird opened sleepy eyes, saw the young man with the callous and grinned. Sleepily he put out his tongue. He filled his chest with air and sang, but softly.

"Charging Elephant Fell On His Face In Front Of An Antelope!"

The sleepy mass heaved, chuckled, giggled; but softly, as at a joke well-worn. The boy by Beautiful Bird grinned at the young man with the callous then snuggled closer to his lover. Beautiful Bird, his eyes shut, but the grin still on his face, put out his tongue.

Charging Elephant looked away and took his hand from his calloused ankle. He said nothing. He stared down over his knees at all the gear scattered on the bare earth. He inspected the drum and the three-string bow glumly, looked at the white bone flute laid before his feet. He reached down, took it up and placed it to his lips. He pursed his lips to blow, glanced sideways at the Elder of Elders, then slowly put the flute down again. Behind him, a voice whispered and he could not see which hunter it was.

"Charging Elephant Fell On His Face In Front Of An Antelope——"

Charging Elephant began to talk, urgently.

"There was a stone—the branch is bent, the root twist-ed but not broken—See!"

He leapt to his feet and immediately lurched sideways as his ankle gave. He came down sickeningly on the cal-loused bone, gritted his teeth, and began to walk up and down before the other Leopard Men, clumsily. The youth who lay in the Elder of Elder's bosom unbroke his voice for a moment and squeaked in delight——

"Chimp!"

The Elder of Elders jerked up, struck the youth a fierce smack on his backside so that the boy yelled at the top of his voice for the pain. But there was noise from the young men too—snorts and gurgles, there were heaving chests and shaking shoulders. There was another fierce smack and wail from the other side of the group; slowly the noise and movement died away to be interrupted every now and then by a fresh snort or gurgle—and once, by an outright guffaw.

Chimp stood still, wearing his new name. A flush swept up under his brown skin, paled, then came flooding back again. He bent his knees, little by little, and felt with his hands for the place where he would sit, without looking for it. He squatted. His mouth was dropped open, his eyes and his nostrils wide. His face stayed dusky red.

The sun moved over the tree and down, the shadow of the leaves crept back towards the bole. Chimp squatted where he was and did not sleep. The red had faded from his face but he did not lay his cheek down on his knees. Instead, he looked bleakly across the plain.

Mountains surrounded the plain on all sides. Here and there were white patches against their light blue. Lower down the blue changed to dark blue, then blue and brown. Below that again was the green of the forested foothills, but Chimp looked through it all. Only when a black storm crept into view, crawling along the mountains on his left, did he watch it and fumble for his flute. But after a moment he let the flute alone and watched the storm cloud without expression. It was so far away it passed like a snail along the mountains. Where it passed, there were flashes and dazzles lower down so that the stormcloud left a glittering snail trail behind it. He watched the cloud drag its smears of falling rain right out of sight; and his own eyes were full of tears so that the plain and the foothills swam.

The sunlight moved inward. A casual breeze elected to drift their way so that the big tree stirred its leaves, woke, roared and was silent again. The Leopard Men began to wake too. They yawned and stretched, and licked furred lips. They stood up and collected a miscellany of things. The Elder of Elders refastened the strings of blown eggshells round his neck. Chimp thrust his flute through his belt. Stooping Eagle smoothed the strings of a bolas with his fingers and inspected the stones, as if lying there, they might have changed while he slept. No one smiled or laughed.

The Elder of Elders had finished with his gear. He waited, frowning and staring round, as the others fixed pouches and shoulder bags and tightened the strings of their loinguards. When all were done and waiting, he stood for a while, his ear cocked at the plain. He laid a finger to his lips and pointed with his spear. Soundlessly, youths, young men, elders, the Leopard Men crept forward through the long grass of the plain.

Droves of animals were grazing over it, knee or shoulder deep in grass. Here and there, between the herds, thorn bushes, termite cities or huge trees like the one they had slept under broke the expanse; but otherwise, it was flat grassland, that washed right up to the forests of the foothills. The Leopard Men entered this plain in single file along a narrow trail that animals had made. They went at the exact speed that threatened no creature. Firefly led the way, crouched and keen. When he reached a point where there were herds on three sides of them, the file stopped as one man. Even Chimp stopped, though by now he was a little way behind the others. The Elder of Elders stared round, saw not only what grazed where, but examined each animal in turn, fat, thin, old, young, healthy, diseased, male, female. Zebras, wild cattle, antelopes, gazelles, rhinos —he saw them all, and knew how they lay, between the invisible ravines with their puddles and their cliffs of clay. He saw, he knew what animal might be trapped against the edge of a cliff or driven over it. So when he turned to his left, the whole file turned and faced the nearer foothill, remembering the dry ravine that lay between it and them. It was a delicate balance, this inserting of a group of men into those societies to a point where a single animal might be cut out. Softly they moved when the Elder moved, aiming without conscious thought, yet nevertheless aiming for the exact point which threatened no herd in particular. Between them and the ravine were three separate droves—but also intermingled at the edges—droves of cattle, zebras, gazelles. As the Leopard Men moved, the margin for error became smaller. Animals on watch lifted their heads and stood at gaze. The expertise was to find a way at which the lookouts would wonder and watch, without knowing which herd was threatened—be wary but not frightened. This wariness was as yet no more than a slight intensification of the normal state of dread. So the herds began to move, grazing slowly into comfortable areas where the threat would be small enough to be ignored. The zebras moved to the left, the cattle to the right. The gazelles, willing to go with neither, moved a little farther off towards the edge of the ravine. The hunters stopped moving. There were many animals in front of them—animals that would escape past, as water escapes from cupped fingers, leaving no more than a drop in the palm. For the hunters were at least ten paces apart; and if the last animal did not leap into space over the edge of the ravine, it could burst between them. That was why each hunter was now hefting his spear gently in the palm of his right hand—why each left hand felt at the strings of the bolas hanging at each belt. It would be a desperate moment when the last animal obeyed nothing but terror. If it should choose to fly through or over the line, there would be a moment of screams and shouts, of whirling bolases and spears with points of fire-hardened wood but stone-weighted, bolas stones whirling in planetary movement at the ends of their strings. An eye might go, or teeth. There might be a broken arm or leg, or even a smashed skull.

Then, with skill and some luck, there would be a kicking hysterical thing threshing about in the grass and a line of light brown men closing in on it.

So the line of Leopard Men halted in the grass and readied their weapons as the animals sifted away. The movement was still slow, as if the herds possessed some statistical sense of the danger and knew there was little threat to each animal, but death for one. The hunters began to move forward again and the animals moved a little more quickly but in caution, not fear. The hunters were like the bows of a ship moving among pack ice, where the white sheets drift away, not struck precisely, but nudged, or even moved apart by a transmitted urging of the water.

The hunters quickened their pace. Now each moved nothing but his legs that were hidden by grass, as if the watching eyes could be deceived into thinking they came no closer. And now the hunters started to run, at the exact point where most was to be gained on the confused and unwary, least lost by a show of open purpose. The herds bellowed and snorted and poured away so that the plain shook under them and dust rose up among the dry grass. Faster the hunters, faster the herds, louder the hooves, panic and squeals——

"Olly-olly-olly-olly!"

It would be trapped and timid gazelles—gazelles harmless and witless and helpless with no aid but their slender legs; gazelles voiceless and delicate, darting this way and that, cannoning into each other, leaping in the air more than the height of a man. Most of them looped away in great arcs, touching the earth only to rebound from it. The bolases were swinging free, the spears were at shoulder height. The last of the gazelles blundered and crashed, the last one of all, left alone between the depth of the ravine and the screaming men and whirling stones. It fled to the brink and back. A spear whipped over it and vanished down the ravine. It leapt vertically as another spear followed the first. It came down, darted to the side, where a figure ran late and clumsily into line. The figure lifted its spear then fell sideways in the grass. The gazelle rose in a great loop over the figure in the grass and went looping away into the plain. Between the semicircle of hunters and the ravine nothing moved at all.

Stooping Eagle ran forward to the fallen figure. He beat one fist into the other as he glared down.

"You, you—Chimp!"

Beautiful Bird looked down into the ravine.

"Now Beautiful Bird must fly down for his spear!"

"And Furious Lion!"

"And Firefly!"

The hunters drew together by the edge of the ravine. They sang, and scowled. The Elder of Elders pointed to a scree of tumbled earth that reached up to not much more than a spear's length below them. One by one, they jumped down into it, they laboured on through loose earth to the bottom, where the spears stuck among puddles in the wet mud. Chimp got himself up slowly on his spear. He was biting his lower lip and grimacing with pain. He did not follow the other hunters. Instead, he went anxiously along the edge of the ravine, looking for an easier way down. The thunder of the herds had diminished to a grumble and died right away. He found nothing but a path so dizzy and narrow that he paused and looked down at the hunters before he took it. The boy called Dragonfly was kneeling by a pool and sipping delicately from his cupped hand. Beautiful Bird was washing the blood off himself while the others stood round and admired his long tears and scratches. Chimp looked up the ravine, but it was so crooked that the corner very little farther up was all he could see. He resigned himself to the dizzy path and began to let himself down it, one hand on the dry, clay cliff, the other feeling for support with his spear. But when he was the height of two men from the bottom the path ended. The last thing that had passed that way had leapt down and in leaping thrust with its hind legs so that the clay cliff had broken away. Without consciously putting these things together, Chimp knew what was the last animal that had used the path and his hair prickled. He stared down into the ravine, his nostrils wide. He saw a paw mark in mud and a tiny smear of blood where the thing had put down its kill to drink. He knew it all at once. Somewhere up the ravine or farther, there would be a cave or perhaps a convenient tree. A creature, a gazelle, perhaps, would hang dead and half-eaten among the branches. The killer would laze there in the sun, fullfed, and licking its paws. Chimp's face went sallow, then dusky red. His breathing came short. He opened his mouth to sing and made nothing but a clucking noise. He took a deep breath and sang out.

"Leopard!"

The hunters snatched up their weapons and turned, then froze, staring up at him. Chimp, one hand against the crumbling cliff, pointed down with his spear.

"Leopard! He has eaten!"

Dragonfly giggled and Stooping Eagle gave a shaky laugh. The hunters moved together, shoulder to shoulder. Their legs quivered. The Elder of Elders went forward, following the indication of Chimp's spear. He squatted, smelt first the paw mark, then the blood. He took his weight off one hand, touched the blood with his finger then tasted it. He glanced up the ravine towards the corner, moved forward a little and examined a mark so small that only he could see it. His face was expression-less, but he breathed as quickly as Chimp. He turned round and ran back to the other hunters. He seized one of the Elders by the wrists and stared into his face. For a moment they were both still and silent. Then the next they were clutching each other, chest to chest and laugh-ing. Dragonfly stood by them. He held his spear with two fists. His mouth was open and his teeth chattering. He got his lips together but only forced the chatter into his body, which shook.

107

The Elder of Elders let his friend go. He was expressionless again. He summoned the hunters with his eyes, looking at each in turn. It was as if he bound them together. He turned and began to move silently up the ravine, through the muddy pools, and the group came with him. The young hunters flanked him, the youths and the other elders were at his back. All crouched low, with spears at the ready. So alike were they, that they might have shared one face between them, a face proud, fearful and glad.

Chimp sang out on the cliff, misery creating an exactness of words for him.

"Wait for me!"

He looked at the distance to the bottom of the ravine, bared his teeth and let go the cliff, to jump. But even as he bent his knees, he became aware of a difference in the air, a faint noise, new, unidentifiable. No herd of animals ever rushed so—and now louder, from higher up the ravine, louder, nearer—he stared at the corner and the hunters stopped, uncertain in their fear and pride, and stared too. They recoiled, lost pride and gladness and kept only fear and uncertainty, they moved aimlessly and clutched each other. The noise became a mighty roar. A mad creature of clods and branches, of trapped animals and rolling stones, of muddy water and foam burst round the corner of the ravine like a monstrous paw. It reared and roared higher than a man. It took the hunters, elders, men, and youths, included them, turned them upside-down, whirled them round, washed away weapons and strength. It beat ringing heads against stones, bounced faces in mud, twisted limbs like straws. It was mindless, resistless and overwhelming. And then the front wave of the flashflood was past, the roar diminishing to a vast, pouring sound. The water smoothed, washed sideways up the crumbling walls of the ravine, accepted the falling clods, beat together down the centre and poured on, the colour of wet earth streaked with yellow foam. Furious Lion was swept along arseupward and only the wriggling of his hams told how he struggled to get upright. The Elder of Elders was clutching into the mud of the cliff and coughing up dark water. A fall of earth knocked him down again. The water sank to no more than knee height. Beautiful Bird stood up and staggered back as a green snake wriggled past him. Dragonfly sat up, hiccuping and howling. The Elder of Elders appeared again farther down the ravine. Again he was expressionless, but this time because his face could not be seen for mud. Then the flood lay still, circling here and there but only ankle deep. There was the sound of Leopard Men splashing and wading and the plop! plop! of falling clods.

A third of the way up the cliff, Chimp squatted high and dry. His mouth was wide open as he looked down from one hunter to the other. They were moving towards each other, wordlessly. Chimp burst into a cackle of laughter. He beat his hands on his knees so that he nearly fell. He leaned his head back and the tears ran down his face. He screamed his laughter and when the breath was out of him he hooted like a woman in labour. The hunters looked up at him evilly through mud and smeared hair. He got some breath and sang.

"We are the Fish Men! Rah! Rah! Rah!"

Beautiful Bird tore one bedraggled feather from his head and held it out.

"How can Beautiful Bird fly now?"

He burst into tears and they made light brown streaks down his face. Stooping Eagle snatched up a handful of mud and hurled it. At once, they were throwing and shouting. A clod with a stone in it hit Chimp on the shoulder. He stopped laughing and grabbed at the cliff again. He sang out at the top of his voice.

"Charging Elephant Who Fell On His Face Before An Antelope would leopard leap but the root is twisted, the bough bent——"

"You—Chimp!"

Stooping Eagle was fumbling at his waist. He got the bolas free and began to swing it round his head, whirr, whirr. Furious Lion scrabbled at the cliff, got himself up a little way then slid down again in a shower of clods. The stones of the bolas came whirling up the cliff face and the wave of their passing was like a shock on Chimp's skin. He scrambled, fast and indignant to the top of the cliff and could see the hunt climbing up under his arm. He ran, angrily and clumsily away through the grass and did not stop until he was out of spear cast. He turned and looked back but the hunters were climbing over the lip of the cliff, so he ran on, then stopped and turned again. They were all there, grouped together. They sang out at him and each other, they gesticulated. He saw Firefly shake his fist. Beautiful Bird had his face in his hands, while Stooping Eagle put an arm round his shoulder. Chimp spread his arms wide, his head on one side, trying to communicate at that distance a complex of feeling for which words were useless.

Furious Lion made throwing gestures with his spear.

"Go away!"

Rutting Rhino put his hands to his face and sang through them.

"We don't like you any more!"

Beautiful Bird lifted his face from his hands and sang as if his heart was breaking.

"Beautiful Bird wanted to fly!"

Stooping Eagle kissed him. A hunter—Chimp could not see who it was—cupped his hands round his face.

"Join the other Chimps!"

There was a howl of laughter. It did not sound kind. Chimp snarled at the distant group and made gestures with his spear, then brought it down again. They were turning away, they were moving along the edge of the ravine, deeper into hunting country. Their backs were to him. He moved after them, but as if they knew what he was doing, they turned a blur of faces towards him and a high-pitched voice stopped him in his tracks.

"Fight the Boss Chimp!"

He heard laughter again; and even at the distance, he could see a youth doing the Boss Chimp walk, erect and clumsy. Slowly the group diminished to a few shocks of dark hair, then passed out of sight.

All this time, Chimp stood at gaze, his mouth open, his eyes blinking occasionally. The hunters were well out of sight when he moved. He dashed his spear into the ground, then snatched it out. He ran forward a few steps, then reeled. He knelt slowly, feeling his ankle without looking at it. He looked only at the place where the hunters had been. He bowed forward, his head between his hands. He put his forehead to the ground. He burst into tears. He howled. He rocked to and fro, up and down, in the flattened grass and when he had cried as much as there was crying in him, he thrust out his legs and lay there, his face against the crushed stems.

The shadows and cries of birds roused him at last. They were returning to roost and talking over the affairs of the day as they went. To Chimp, their message was plain and urgent. He knelt up with a jerk and stared at the red mess of the sunset. He leapt to his feet and whirled round as if there might be a leopard behind him—then whirled round again and reeled. In the warm air, goosepimples rose all over his skin. He clenched and bared his teeth—and when he let them apart for a moment they chattered. He began to run after the hunting group, but stopped, then ran in a circle. He stopped again and gripped himself with his arms. Tears chased each other down his face but he made no sound. A problem was all round him and through him but he had no word for it, nothing was like it, he had never had a problem to solve before. He was neither sick nor old; but he was alone.

Opposite the sunset a white shoulder pushed up over the mountains. She rose as was natural, over the Place of the Women, far away. Chimp knew she was fully with child and she did not add to his fear. She neither threatened nor invited, but was placidly sunk in her own business and allowed men to hunt. But as Chimp peered round through the changing light he found no comfort for he heard the noises of animals increase at her rising. She allowed them to hunt too. He settled to a clumsy trot through the grass. As if some instinct had been triggered, he aimed blindly towards where he knew there was higher ground—over there, through the milky light, where the ravine opened out to a wide water hole and the rocks of the foothills began. The stones of his bolas thumped on his thigh and he gripped his spear as if it were the wrist of a friend. The Sky Woman rose higher, floated free. Far away over the plain he heard the scream of a gripped zebra and he reeled as he ran. The Sky Woman flooded him with her light and ignored him. He staggered to a halt and knelt in the grass. His mouth was wider open and sweat streamed off him. He stayed there, and for a while heard nothing but his heart. He collapsed on the ground, his face sideways, his breath stirring up little

113

clouds of dust. Before his face, he saw how the last dregs of redness had faded from the mountains where the sun had left them. Blue and green seeped away into the earth. The hyaenas and the hunting dogs were out. He heard them and he saw them. There were eyes everywhere, like sparks of cold fire. He got up and began to make his way forward again. He no longer ran but darted then stopped and looked and listened. The ground fell away to the waterhole and as he came near there was a sudden flurry, plunging, snorting and the clatter and rumble of hooves as the animals that had been drinking there fled away. He shuddered and bared his teeth.

Yet he was safe though he had no way of knowing it. He brought with him the menace of a whole line of light brown creatures that struck from afar; and to those with little thought or no thought at all, his mere appearance was enough. So safely he stole forward and upward into the shade of rocks and trees, and presently, the shadow of a high cliff. It was not vertical and he laboured up it from knot to crevice, where the indignant birds squawked and beat their wings at an intruder; or admitting inequality, dropped from their eyries and flapped heavily into the light.

III

The settlement stayed as wide awake as the animals on the plain. It was not merely that the children had had a sleep in the middle of the day and now played on into the sunset, for they always did that. It was rather that Palm knew, and the women with her, what shape the Sky Woman would be in when she rose. It was a later rising than for the Leopard Men, for the Hot Springs were in the shadow of the mountain. So the women strolled for a while in blue twilight. They did not talk much, though they moved in groups. Every now and then, there would come a sudden burst of laughter in the twilight. The woman with child hooted more regularly and with abandon, in her shelter.

Palm stood once more by the topmost pan where the water boiled and the vapour hung. She watched one part of the mountain outlined darkly against the deepening blue of the evening sky. Below her, by the river, the women had their arms about each other's waists and necks, or waited in groups from which the bursts of laughter or giggles rose, but she paid no attention to them. A fire burned brightly before one shelter where the woman was in labour, but she ignored it and the hooting of the woman. She stood there, not her own length from the boiling water. Her fists were clenched, and she yearned up at the dark outline.

Children began to scream by the river. They had passed to the state where they did not know how tired they were. They fought and howled. She heard how the women went to them and tried to quieten them. Somewhere, a baby was whining and some booby of a boy crying his eyes out. Suddenly there was no more laughter from the women but firm words. She heard how they shoo'd the children, collected them, brought them to the rocks; and the children quietened, with the occasional spat from sheer exhaustion. Presently there was no human sound at all except the regular hooting. In a dozen huts or shelters or lean-tos the children were being told how this night of nights they must not come out till sunup, because of the dreams that walked. Palm yearned at the mountain, and panted, her mouth wide open.

There was a change in the sky. Just over the dark outline and in the expected place, the blue of the sky was lightening. She watched, until the water in her eyes blurred everything so that she swung on her heel and blinked them clear. Half the plain and the mountains that surrounded it were drenched in milky light that moved closer and closer to the river and the settlement. The women were coming out into the open from their homes again. She saw flashes and glossy loops wake as the light moved across the river, fast as girls could wade in line with a net. The light touched the nearer bank. The trees round the Place of Women grew a foliage of pale shells and ivory sprays. Down there, the women stood, silent, and waiting for their shadows. Palm turned and stared up. A tiny grain of white pushed up over the rim of the mountain, the curve of a white shoulder. She lifted her hands high and cried out again and again. The white washed her, the shells were startling white against her brown skin, her eyes flashed like ice. Below her the women stood, the light pale on their faces. The Sky Woman swung free of the mountain.

Palm lowered her hands to her sides. The moon fell into the boiling water and danced there, broke up, re-formed, then broke again, as if the water were cool as the river. The women were laughing and chattering. She heard a high giggle, near to hysteria, a little scream, then a squeak and more giggles. She thought to herself—they believe everything is settled! They can start licking their lips——

At once, the necessity was back. She saw it more clearly than the light dancing in the water, a shell full of the dark, compelling drink. She smelt it and caught her breath. It was there, nowhere, everywhere, close; and there was darkness behind it. She shut her eyes and her mouth, clenched her fists. She was trembling. The woman in labour hooted again.

When Palm opened her eyes, she no longer trembled, and the shell of drink had gone somewhere else with its

117

smell. She stared at the Sky Woman and a kind of bleak certainty fell over her like a cold wind. She moistened her lips and she spoke to herself as she always did when the cold wind came.

"The Sky Woman is just the Sky Woman. That is all. To think anything else is to be young—is to think like a man——"

She turned round. The light had reached the Lodge of the Leopard Men below her and some of the leopard skulls gleamed with light. She saw only the front row of them but knew where the others lay, the older skulls, yellowed and falling apart, those at the very back, little more than two rows of fangs and teeth. All at once, as if the cold wind that had fallen on her had done something to her eyes, she saw the Lodge for what it was, without the distortion of contempt or humour or caution. It was a pan like all the others but empty of water. The pan had grown and grown as pans did, the water leaving layer after layer of the yellow and white stony substance at the lips; and then by some necessity of the earth—a cooling of the water, perhaps—the water had cut an escape—there, at the narrow entrance where the curtain of leopard skin closed it. Nor had that ended the business; for at the inner end of the pan another had started to grow but stopped, when the water had abandoned the whole place in favour of a string of pans higher up. Her moment of seeing was as clear and precise as if she had woken from a dream and found nothing but the factual straws by her cheek.

The woman hooted. Palm made herself graceful and smiling. She swayed down from the boiling water. Hands up for balance, her long hair moving gently in the wind of her descent, she came down to the level space. The women ran to her.

"Palm! Palm! When shall we begin?"

Gracefully she walked between them towards the Woman's Place and smiled on this girl and that.

"When there is a naming."

The girls broke into passionate speech but she paid no heed. The older women said nothing, but watched her as she paced towards the trees and entered in. She reached the curtains of hide that were sewn everywhere with shells, the mere sight of which would send a man crouching away in dread. She lifted the curtain and went in. The place was dark because of the trees that stood so close round it, but there was light enough on the open side from the moonlit waters of the river. Two women stood by the river's edge, outlined against it and working at the contraption that stood between them. The scent of what it held reeked into the air. It was a full-bellied skin, held in a tripod of strong boughs. The women were stirring this and singing softly. When they saw her, they stood back. She came close, leaned down and sniffed so that the reek took her in the throat and she started trembling again. The Brewing Woman handed her a stick.

"It is ready."

Throatily, Palm muttered in the reek.

119

"We will wait."

The Bee Woman looked up.

"Wait? Till when?"

Throatily again, heart beating fast, darkness all around.

"Till there is a name."

The women glanced at each other but said nothing. Do I try to stop myself, she said, inside her head. Do I grasp at anything? And do I—would I rather there were—than—I must! Oh I must!

She stirred the liquid with the stick, moved aside the bubbles and cream and yearned down at the dark stuff, the stuff so like the darkness behind the shell. The Bee Woman hiccuped then sniggered. Palm glanced up at her.

"Try it, Palm. You have to try it!"

The Brewing Woman reached down, scooped up a coconut shell full of reeking stuff and held it out.

"Try it."

After all, she thought, I have to. It is my duty. Nothing can be plainer than that. Even if there is no naming, still I have to try it, to make sure——

She put the shell to her lips and sipped elegantly. At once, the necessity was clear, was there, was kind, even.

"It's good."

The two women were laughing with her. They had shells.

"It *is* good. Very good!"

She lifted her face with the shell and drained it down. She was full of warmth and quiet happiness. She heard a great cry from the shelter and she knew suddenly that though the Sky Woman was just the Sky Woman, it did not matter and there would be a naming, yes, a naming, then a midnight feast. The cry had hardly died away when she had begun to move towards the curtains, knowing that it was the birth cry and all would be well. She went quickly from the trees and again the women watched her but this time they said nothing. Quickly she hurried to the shelter, ducked her head and went in. The woman was lying back, her damp face collapsed and moved only by the light of the fire. A helper was by her on one side, wiping her forehead and on the other side another helper was working at the bitten and knotted string, and the child. She heard the Namer enter, turned and held it out. Palm took it, a girl, turned it, held it up by the legs, poked, pried, counted. She knelt and laid it in her lap. The child squirmed with all its body and made mewing sounds. The helper handed her a splinter of wood. She thrust it into the fire until it burst into flame, moved the flame to and fro in front of the dark, unfocused eyes till she saw them try to follow. She threw the stick in the fire and cradled the baby. Her breasts throbbed and hurt. Laughing, she put her face on the downy head. A hand closed round her little finger and held it hard. She laughed again in the face of the mother.

"She has a name! Do you hear me, Windflower? Your daughter has a name! She is Little Palm!"

She leaned forward and placed the child in the mother's

arms and they moved to receive it. Windflower managed a smile with her damp lips. She Who Names The Women squatted back, then ducked out under the hanging skins. The women were there in a crowd. They said nothing but waited.

"Little Palm!" she cried, understanding how the name had chosen the child. "She is Little Palm!"

After that, there was nothing but laughter and singing. Some of the women hurried away to the place by the river, others drifted upward to the hot pans, some crowded to the mother and new baby.

Palm walked breathlessly among them, back to the Place of Women, where the drink reeked before the happy darkness. Her breasts ached, and she laughed. She spoke aloud.

"I am not too old to bear another child."

IV

In the moon-drenched hunting country, the business of
the animals was in full swing. But in the forested foothills there was little to be done, and nothing to be done
at all on the bare cliffs. Life went on noisily in the tree
tops, among birds and apes. But the cliffs seemed to
hold no life at all, for the birds had either returned to
their eyries, or had flown out in the light air across the
plain to mingle with the bird societies by the waterholes.
There was only one place of visible life—two sparks that
appeared every now and then, when Chimp shifted his
head. He squatted high up on a ledge where only the
birds could get at him; and they did not want to. His
spear stood against the rocks at his right hand and his
bone flute lay on the ledge beside the spear where he
had put it down as if it were no more to him than a
stick. Every now and then, he stroked his ankle as he
looked this way or that. He was still unaware that he
had a problem to solve. He felt nothing but anger and
grief. Instinct had bidden him remedy this by eating. So
at first he had squatted, gnawing the dried fish that the
women had provided for him. Yet this was not proper
food but only stuff to be eaten in extremity. In itself, it

was advertisement of the fact that the eater had some-how failed to be a man. It added humiliation to what he felt already. He got no good of it and he had given up the attempt to eat so that he was at a loss again. The hunting group drew him and repelled him at the same time. He shouted aloud.

"Fish men! The girls take you in their nets!" Because anger was so much easier to bear than humiliation he dwelt on them, sneering at the plain. They would, his mind said, in its man's way, have grown the fireflower and set a necklace of hunters round it. He saw them in his mind with a sudden precision that brought back a wave of grief. He moaned and writhed his body as if the grief were a physical pain. Yet there was nothing else to think of; and his mind, once turned that way would go nowhere else. It examined the fire, the broken, toasted meat, the laughter, the singing. He saw Furious Lion beat at his little drum, he watched Stooping Eagle strum his three-stringed bow. He saw Chimp there too, happily tootling away on his bone flute. At that, the mixture of Chimp being there and here too, satisfactorily there and unsatis-factorily here, turned the pain to gross anguish, so that he wailed aloud and a nearby roosting bird flapped and squawked. He saw them singing, heard them singing.

"A-hunting we will go, a-hunting we will go!"

The Chimp that was here, turned his head to the left

and searched the farther plain, the forest, the slopes of the foothills for a spark of fire or a wisp of smoke. He snatched up his flute, put it to his lips, then threw it down again. The whole world under the Sky Woman was swimming in the water of his eyes. He heard the Elder of Elders singing in his deep, happy voice as Chimp tootled with him. They were all singing and clapping, bawling the song of the Sky Woman in triumph——

> *"You are not upright and bitter,*
> *You do not lie on your back and moan,*
> *Oh whitebummed, bigbellied skywoman,*
> *Leave us alone!"*

And then again they sang——

> *"A-hunting we will go! A-hunting we will go!*
> *Rah! Rah! Rah!"*

And now, fullfed, they were turning towards sleep and each other. Dragonfly, who had been a boy so little time ago—Ripe Apple—Beautiful Bird and Charging Elephant Fell On His Face Before An Antelope—the calm authority of the Elder of Elders—the two other elders who were never apart——

Chimp that was here moaned and again the tears spilled down his face. Chimp that was there reached out a hand to Dragonfly who smiled back; but Furious Lion seized the lovely boy by the ankle. Beautiful Bird stood up clumsily, walked like the Boss Chimp and the Elder of Elders laughed. Chimp beat his fists on his knees. All at once, it was like the bursting of a storm cloud in his head, mighty wind, flash of fire. He sang out of the pain inside him.

"I am Leopard Who Struck With His Water Paw!"

He was the Leopard of all Leopards, huge and lithe. He was made of moonlight and fire. He stalked through the forest with writhing tail, teeth bared and eyes like the lightning. He came towards them out of the darkness and they howled with fear. They fell on their knees begging for mercy, but saw there was none, and ran. Dragonfly knelt pitiably, he was too afraid to run. He had become a boy again, tender and delicate and fearful. The Leopard of all Leopards seized him in its teeth and he shrieked with fear. The leopard left the hunters to cower behind the trees and bore the boy away into the darkness——

Charging Elephant was the mightiest elephant there ever was. His herd spread far and wide over the plain. They acknowledged him. He was Boss Elephant. Among the males he was as a man among boys, as an Elder of Elders among women. His head was above all the herd. His ears gave them shade, with his tusks he uprooted huge trees. When he trumpeted the mountains answered but all else was silent. His feet were the terror of things with teeth and claws. Even the Leopard of all Leopards, the Leopard With The Water Paw, stole away when he heard those feet on the hard earth. Charging Elephant went forward to clear the world. He came to the forest's edge. He tore aside the boughs and his eyes flashed fire at what he saw within. They were hunters, little men, and they had killed, for Charging Elephant saw the hacked feet of his cow beside their fire. He trumpeted and the mountains answered. He tore whole trees out of the way, he made a path of crushed rock. The Elder of Elders leapt into a tree and yelled with terror, but Charging Elephant tore up the tree by the roots and hurled tree and Elder over the mountains together. He knelt on Beautiful Bird and Furious Lion! Dragonfly lay on his face, shaking and weeping. Charging Elephant left him till last. He knelt with his oaken knees on Firefly and Rutting Rhino—he knelt on the last of the hunters, a man with a calloused ankle and a bone flute in his hand! Blood burst out of the man's mouth——

Chimp that was here leapt to his feet and yelled as if he had been struck with a whole bunch of thorns. Then he was falling, falling, down, down, scraping and bumping. He grabbed at rocks with his hands and felt his skin tear. His feet found lodgment and he stayed, his face sideways against stone. The birds were swirling and crying round him.

Gradually the birds went and there was nothing but a silent place, made of stone and milky light. He licked his torn fingers and inspected the dark blood on his knees. Below him, his spear and his bone flute lay in a bush where his involuntary movement had knocked them. He climbed down, thrust the bone flute through his belt and took the spear in his left hand. He waited, staring round him over the forest and the plain. The Sky Woman sat in the very top of her tree. All at once, he knew that the hunting group was there somewhere, far off and indifferent. He knew that he was one thing by itself, Chimp That Is Here. Feelings swelled in his belly as if he were with child of them. They overwhelmed. He lifted up his voice and howled at the mountains and the Sky Woman, at the forests and the plain, as if he were not a Leopard Man but a dog. He was careless of danger and the tears dropped off his face. He howled again and again and the cliff mocked him with its voice. He beat his head with his fist and felt nothing. Even the birds accepted his grief, at the end, without the comment of voice or wing. They did no more than stir in their nests as the dog voice howled and the cliff howled back.

At last he could howl no more. He whimpered instead and the whimper lay on the surface of a grief that was deep as ever. Then, as if something had come to be born, the feelings were clear in their message. They gave him a knowledge, a certainty. He began to run clumsily along below the cliffs; and as he ran, he whimpered.

"Ma! Ma!"

V

The Sky Woman was halfway down her tree, yet so bright was she that she had the sky to herself, save for one icy sparkle of light above the mountains where the sunset had been. Chimp no longer ran fast, but trotted and still whimpered every now and then. He had remembered things that slowed him—one, that when the Sky Woman was in full belly, children went to the huts and stayed there, while unguessable things occupied the girls and the mothers. Moreover he remembered that he had no mother himself, since she had died—accidentally, of course, as so often happened to the daunting, mysterious creatures. This did not matter to him much, and never had; but now, he felt the lack of her without understanding what she might have done to take away this pain. Nor had he a woman of his own, which was unusual, but happened too. Those hunters who had no women thought of it as a stroke of good luck, when they thought of it at all. Yet he was trotting towards the women, drawn, in his extremity; and when he had got so used to the pain that it was a thing there, like a wound, he began to feel a certain caution as if he were a man approaching a lair. His shadow followed him and his foot held up. This too was strange enough but there was a reason for it. He was running along the skirts of rock. Upended strata sloped up from his left to his right. The slope was just enough to force his foot up on the right side, against the weakness. This fact was another that kept him trotting and seemed in some obscure way to be forcing him towards the place where he was no longer wholly certain he wanted to be.

At last he could see the cloud of steam that hung over the Hot Springs. He slowed to a crouching walk that brought his limp back. He held his spear, as if he might have to use it at any moment. He moved towards the river and the open place where the children played. Everything was still, everything silent. He went close, till at last he could hear the ripple of water.

A baby whimpered in one of the shelters, and an old man coughed somewhere, tuss, tuss, tuss. He stood, crouched on the bleached earth and the goosepimples rose all over him. He licked his lips and looked round him slowly, saw the trees round the Place of Women and flinched away. He took a step or two towards the safety of the plain then stopped. Suddenly, for no reason at all, he remembered the Namer of Women and his hair prickled.

The rising vapour above the Hot Springs had changed. It had not changed while he watched; but there was something different about it that had been there all the time he ran through the open space and he had not noticed it before. The Sky Woman shed her light through it and on it, as she shed light on everything. But the vapour was lit from below, as if there were a fire, kindled impossibly in water. From that direction, as from a local sunset, the cloud was coloured dull pink—so dull a pink, the eye could not stay with it, but saw it for a moment then had to wait until the colour seemed to flow back again. And now—as if his ears had gone up there among the pans with his eyes—he heard a faint sound, high and complex. He dismissed this sound because it was impossible, like the fire. He put one foot back and lifted the spear by his shoulder. He began to move forward, hunting fashion. He gulped, and ran forward to the rise where the first pan was, with a white Sky Woman caught in it. He climbed soundlessly; and in each pan, a white Sky Woman danced. He went faster from pan to pan until he reached the open space before the Lodge of the Leopard Men and the pink light of the fire spilled over him so that his face shook.

The leopard skin that had kept the entrance inviolate was down on the rock at his feet. The impossible sound was indeed the laughter of women. He leapt into the entrance and his hair stood up as if he faced a rhino in rut.

The fire burned on the floor in the middle of the pan and the women lay, squatted, lounged round it. In his first glimpse—a glimpse that froze everything like a lightning flash—he saw two girls, little more than children, holding leopard skulls with two hands against their mouths. The noise, the babble, screech, giggle, chatter, scream, was brighter than the fire. Opposite him, and leaning against the inner pan where the leopard skulls had been, was She Who Names The Women, Namer of Women, She Whose Heart is Loaded Down With Names. She held a skull in her right hand. She held it by its fangs and liquid ran out of it. She was leaning back, one hand supporting her. She was laughing and the light of the fire flowed in her eyes through her tangled hair. She saw him, she screamed with laughter. She lifted the skull in her hand over her shoulder with a woman's gesture and hurled it at him. The skull flipped sideways out of the pan, the length of a man from his face. He cried out, half in outrage, half in terror.

"No!"

But there were faces turned towards him, firelit faces, faces moon-whitened, with sparkling eyes, white teeth and a maze of floating hair. Shrieks, laughter and words rose together.

"A man! A man!"

They were tumbling over each other, foul stuff spilling from scattered skulls so that the fire spat, hissed and died down. Faces rose up among the shrieks and hands clutched at him. He threatened the faces with his spear, dropped it, then stumbled back and fled. He found himself only a pace from the boiling water and only just swayed round it. He ran down to the next pan, but the laughter and the white faces were there, so that he turned back. He blundered into a knot of soft flesh that would not be untied. There was noise, there were arms of blunt flesh that wound round him like the strings of a bolas. They were screeching to him and to each other. His belt and loin-guard went away as if they themselves had elected to. He was being forced down and there was more soft flesh to receive him. His loins refused them in hatred and dread; but their hands were clever, so clever, so cruel, so cunning. In the noise he heard his own cry of pain fly up and up——

"Hoo-oo-oo-oo!"

Up and up his cry went away from the pain that stayed behind between his legs and stiffened him. He was down on the soft flesh, the soft wetness and terror of teeth. Half of him tried to get away from the terror and the weight of soft arms holding him down; and half of him was thrusting and jerking like an animal wounded in the spine. Then he and sheness entered the dreadful place and cried out together and small teeth met in his ear. But there might be teeth, there would be teeth waiting in that wet place and when half his body had jerked its will, he tore himself away. The arms allowed him for a moment but then they caught him again.

"Me! Me!"

Shrieks, laughter, babble, and the merciless skill of hands——

"Hoo-oo-oo-oo!"

There was no way out, but through, compelled to go once more into the place of darkness where the wet flesh had its will. Then he lay, his ears singing among the white women sprawled on rocks, the laughing, hiccuping girls. He felt blood on his neck, tasted it in his mouth. The woman smell was all round, hung on his flesh, hung in his beard and under his nostrils. He tried to get up but his arms and legs were held. A white leopard skull was approaching his face backwards, he turned his face away from the foul smell in the skull. It was forced against his mouth and he clenched his teeth and pressed his lips together. But a hand stole over his forehead and two fingers closed on his nose so that his mouth gaped open for air. His ears sang so that he could hardly hear their laughter; and then the dreadful liquid was slopped in his mouth. He gulped and gagged and struggled against blunt flesh but more liquid slopped in, more and more so that his chest contracted and blew the last of it out in spray. Then he collapsed back against rock, faint, in the binding arms, the laughter, the unmeaning talk, the kisses, small bites and caresses. A hand came from nowhere and wiped his face with hair.

There was silence, except for the singing in his ears. He hiccuped like a white girl and opened his eyes. Someone was approaching over the rocks and the Sky Woman lit her softly from the side. She came swaying, her long grass skirt rustling, the shells making a tiny noise on her breast. She staggered once in her swaying, but still came on towards him. Hair draggled over one side of her face and was caught among the shells. She was laughing without a sound and her eyes were dark and seemed to take the

134

marrow from his bones. She came closer and the women who held him giggled as if the joke would never end. She was beginning to kneel down between his feet. She knelt, laughing soundlessly, leaned forward on her left hand and her hair fell on his thigh.

He cried out.

"No!"

The giggles turned to laughter and the hands held him fast. She shot out her right hand like a snake.

"Hoo-oo-oo-oo!"

When he came down with his cry, back down to the rocks and arms, something had happened—and not between his legs. The foul-smelling drink had warmed itself in his belly. He could feel it glowing and about to burn. It sent up a flame that reached nearly inside his head. Another leopard skull appeared, backwards and pressed against his mouth, another hand closed his nose. He gulped and gulped again, then blew out another spray. The fire shot up and the inside of his head was visited by a puff of flame. Suddenly, he understood that he had never noticed how beautiful She Who Names The Women was, how exquisite and exciting was her smell, how white and young her body, how clever and to be consented to, her hands! The women were letting him go and laughing and he heard himself laugh with them as the flames licked up round his head and down, warmingly, exhilaratingly between his legs. She was letting him go too; and laughing, he seized her hand to put it back. But she avoided him gently then beckoned. Another skull appeared and he shook his head but she would not be denied. Her soft face with its huge eyes came close to him, she gurgled with laughter, in her voice that was deeper than the voice of girls, and spoke.

"Drink, little Leopard Man!"

It was such a joke and she was so gentle he could do nothing but please her. He gulped again and again, therefore, spluttered and choked. Then they were laughing together, she was holding his hand and pulled him after her. He went with her, on fire, with the world moving round him. Even when he saw where she was leading him he felt no terror. It was as if a ravine had opened between him and his dread of the Women's Place. She lurched against him and it was natural that his arm should go round her waist. She laughed with him and he thought it was the lurch that made her laugh. They came to the barrier of hide sewn with awful shells and he shouted and struck it with his fist. She lifted it and he blundered in. She came behind him, pulled him round. She came close and her laughter gurgled like a little spring. He could see nothing but the glossy water of the river and She Who Names The Women, who was so young and beautiful, outlined against it. She pressed close. She kissed him with her lips and tongue, she laid her breasts against the blood on his chest. His mouth searched after hers when she let him go and he could not find it. He looked round for her but there was nothing to see but a strange shape by

136

the river's edge—a shape from which the foul—but not so foul—smell came reeking. Then he saw her dark figure appear beside it. She thrust her arm in, lifted it, held something to her face and stood there drinking. She took the thing down from her face and threw it—again with the womanish gesture—into the river. She turned round and though the darkness hid her face he knew she was looking for him. She made her body move like a snake from feet to head so that he knew without seeing, her softness and wetness and warmth. He saw the outline of her grass skirt collapse round her feet. She stepped out of it into the darkness and vanished. He looked round him.

"Where are you?"

Her laughter gurgled again, softly, like a little spring. The water comes up with never a bubble, it wells, dances to itself night and day and lets flow a stream of clearness and life for the grasses and the flowers.

"Here."

He knelt down. His head was in the woman smell of her hair and neck. Her warm arms stroked his back, there were no teeth—only dark closenesses into which he throbbed and sank. Thought went from him, and the very possibility of fear. The end was like a beginning, and it merged softly with sleep.

VI

The Sky Woman went down, taking her light with her, and the ripples of the river lit from the other direction. In the trees round the Place of Women, a bird began to strike his incessant note. The ringdoves spoke and the rock pigeons. A fish leapt. The sunlight crept down the trees and touched the hide curtains on one side, slid down, shone from the polished top of a clumsy bench—examined a multitude of shapes, bundles of plants, vessels of coconut shell or bark. The light touched the earth, moved to a foot, an ankle with a callous. It found other feet, warmed a leg, a thigh. Outside the hide curtains the day went about its business in full swing. The sunlight found a face.

Chimp rolled away from the light. He was conscious first of himself, coming from a darkness without dreams, then of himself surrounded by a faint and unaccustomed ache as if he had been too long in the sun. It was the strangeness of these feelings that opened his eyes before he had remembered anything. But when he had opened them his mouth fell open too. There was an unquestionably female back in front of him with black hair straggled over it. He sat up with a jerk, so that the faint ache in his head jerked too, and looked round him. He leapt to his feet.

The Namer of Women groaned, said something and rolled over. She sat up and smeared the hair from her face. She was neither young nor beautiful. The dust of the place was on her face and her body and her hair tangled as a briar. She blinked, put one hand to her forehead and screwed up her face. She opened her eyes again and looked round slowly. Her eyes passed across Chimp, so that he backed away, his hands between his legs. She looked at the tripod with the hanging skin and she went still, as if she were looking at a poisonous snake. She licked her lips and muttered.

"Now you've done it!"

She looked at him with a hatred that lifted the goosepimples on his skin.

"You naked ape!"

He stayed frozen—not even enough in control of himself to be wary. She looked down at her own body and the hatred went out of her face. She bit her lip.

"Two of us."

She got up and went to the edge of the river. She did not sway like a palm, she was not gracious and graceful, she staggered as she went. She took a shell, knelt down, scooped up water and drank again and again. She threw water over her face and body till she dripped with it.

Chimp remembered everything. Devastation fell on him out of the sky. He lay down, his face against the earth. He could not even weep.

Presently he saw feet by his face, and the ends of a grass skirt. Her voice sounded mild.

"Well, we must think what to do. Sit up!"

He rolled over and squatted, his hands still between his legs. He muttered.

"My loinguard——"

The feet went away and he heard her voice by the river.

"How should I know?"

He looked cautiously sideways. She was reaching into the skin that hung from the tripod. She brought up a coconut shell and drank from it. He smelt the stuff, and his face twisted with disgust. He could find no words anywhere and stared down at the ground again. There was a time, while he heard her moving about—heard a rubbing, a washing, the swish of hair. The feet came back, and there was no dust on them. Her skirt rustled and spread on the ground as she knelt in front of him.

"Well? Aren't you going to look at me?"

He lifted his head. She was the Name Giver again, the shells white on her splendid breasts, the hair no longer smeared across her face. The tears welled from his eyes and he said the only words he could find out of the confusion.

"I shall die."

"Come now! Who said anything about dying? Only women die!"

He looked down again.

"I shall die."

A hand touched his arm.

"A mighty hunter die? You might be killed, indeed. It is your glory, is it not? But die! Why—if mighty hunters believed they all died, think how *lonely* they would be! No man could bear it!"

Timidly, he looked up. She was smiling. She was younger once more. Her eyes were young and taking charge of her face. Among all the mysteries and confusions that had overwhelmed him, there rose another—that She Who Names The Women could look at him with a face that was at once smiling and sad.

She patted his arm and spoke as to a child.

"There! Better?"

Some of the confusion left him; and because of this he found indignation stir in him. He opened his mouth to speak, but she saw, and forestalled him.

"You shouldn't have come hunting us poor women when the Sky Woman has a full belly! Who knows what dreams she would send you?"

A little of yesterday's grief came back to him.

"It was none of my fault—they drove me away from the hunt."

"Why?"

The grief swelled.

"The root is warped, the branch twisted! Charging Elephant fell on his face before a gazelle——"

She made an impatient gesture.

"You have a weak ankle. We all know that!"

"The gazelle leapt over me as I fell!"

She squatted back. She frowned and spoke thoughtfully and as if he were not there.

"I understand. You should have gone down the river. But it is very difficult to tell, in these cases where the foot is not turned right over at birth—oh, now, come, Leopard Man!"

She knelt forward and peered into his face.

"You mustn't be frightened! You didn't go down the river! See—the river is there and you are here!"

The grief of yesterday boiled up and swamped everything else. He put his head back, howled, and the tears shot out of his eyes.

"They called me Chimp!"

Then her arms were round him and he was sobbing against her shoulder. Her hands caressed his back.

"There, there!" she said, "there, there, there——"

And all the time, her own shoulders shook.

Presently his sobs died away. She took his smudgy chin in her hands and lifted it.

"They'll forget," she said. "You'll see, my little Leopard Man. Men can forget anything. They'll have a new song or tune or saying. They'll have a new joke to tell over and over again, or a bright stone to show, or a strange flower, or a splendid new wound to boast about. Why—you'll forget your dream, too, won't you?"

"Dream?"

"Last night—all the confusion. The Sky Woman sent it.

142

About the Lodge of the——"

He looked at the ground, glumly.

"I shan't forget."

"Oh yes you will!"

He glanced up briefly, then down again.

"There is too much song—too many leaves in the forest—too many words like dust—they'd never believe it—never. How could they?"

She came close and spoke earnestly.

"Listen, Chi—Listen, Charging Elephant. The Leopard Men wouldn't believe it. You said that."

"Well?"

"Aren't you a Leopard Man?"

"I suppose so."

"Then," said She Who Names The Women, "you can't believe it either, can you?"

Chimp inspected this. There was a long silence.

She sat back, legs tucked under her, weight on one hand, palm spread out. The other hand was making little marks on the ground with the point of one finger. She watched her finger.

"In any case," she said at last, "I don't think I should talk about my dream with the others. Particularly not with Stooping Eagle and Firefly. You see, Stooping Eagle and Cherry, and Firefly and Little Fish——"

"Cherry? Little Fish?"

There was another long silence.

"Well," she said at last. "Well, I see."

The confusion was simplifying in him. It was a dream; and it left him looking at the cruelty of the Leopard Men.

"Clonk."

"What?"

"Clonk. My ankle says clonk."

He looked up at her—for comfort perhaps. But she had turned her head sideways and was staring at the fat bag in its tripod. The wry smile was back. Her words meant nothing.

"And I go clonk inside. But you can't look into a baby's head."

She glanced back at him, then down at her fingers on the earth.

"When I have a baby——"

Instantly the goosepimples were back.

"What is that to do with me?"

"Oh nothing, nothing, of course! The Sky Woman does it all by herself! However, I haven't had a baby since my Leopard Man was killed by the sun. Strange, is it not? But now——"

He tried to understand her.

"Now?"

She sat up and passed a hand over her forehead.

"I have dreams, too. But they mean nothing. Nothing, nothing. *What threatens us?* The Sky Woman is—who knows what she is, or what we are, except that we are like nothing else? Charging Elephant—the dream, your dream——"

144

"Well?"

He saw that she was changing colour, a flush was spreading over her breast, her neck, her cheeks.

"When I brought you here, it was—not wholly bad?"

He remembered the place with no teeth, the darkness that took away fear.

"No. No."

The flush came and went in her cheeks.

"You see—you may—that is—Charging Elephant, you may be my Leopard Man. When you return from the hunt, you may come to the hut and—if you like, that is."

He thought of the Leopard Men, their awe of She Who Names The Women. A great lightness took the place of the grief in him. He spoke gruffly, to hide his new joy.

"If you like."

The flush died away from her cheeks. She knelt forward and spoke with quiet dignity.

"Charging Elephant, you may rub noses."

A girl's voice was crying somewhere beyond the hide curtains.

"Palm! Palm! Oh Palm!"

The Namer Of Women leapt to her feet and went quickly to the curtains.

"Stay outside!"

"Palm!"

"What is it?"

"They are coming back—Palm. The Leopard Men!

145

They are at least a day early, Palm!"

She Who Names The Women stood silent, her hands pressed against her cheeks. She looked quickly at Chimp then took her hands away.

"Listen—Minnow. Tell the others. Clear everything away——"

"We're doing it!"

She Who Names The Women called after her.

"Everything, mind! Not a trace!"

Chimp had begun to move round. He searched over the earth.

"My loinguard—where is it?"

"How should I know! Up by the pans I suppose!"

"I can't——"

"You must go—you *must* go!"

"How? Where?"

"Oh——!"

"Naked!"

"Wait. I'll see how far away they are——"

She hurried through the curtains and the trees, quickly she climbed by the pans. A belt and loinguard lay floating in the first of them. She fished it out, then stared over the plain under her lifted hand. The Leopard Men were nearer even, than Minnow had said. If she had allowed herself to think that her ears were still girl-keen, she could have believed that she heard their chant. Even so, she could see how they walked in single file and how every few paces they jerked their sticks in the air.

146

"Rah! Rah! Rah!" said She Who Names The Women bitterly, "Rah! Rah! Rah!"

She blinked in the light, shaded her eyes more closely. She saw that two of the hunters carried a pole between them. A burden hung from the pole. She examined the size of the burden, the colour——

"Oh changeless Sky Woman! Not *another* leopard!"

She went quickly back to the Place of Women and threw his loinguard at him.

"Put it on and go."

"Where? How?"

She beat her head with her fists.

"Haven't I trouble enough? Go! Jump in the river—then wade along and up through the woods——"

"I'll go——'

"And don't you think I'm going to have a man under my feet all the——"

He went sousing into the water, his loinguard in one hand. He came up and waded, shuddering. The last he saw of her there, she was standing by the tripod with a coconut shell in her hand. Then he was busy in weeds and hanging boughs. He pulled himself up in mud, stood under the trees and dressed himself. When it was secure, he walked casually through the woods and came out on rocks. He sidled round the settlement, up by the Hot Springs in the rising vapour, then down the other side. He could see the procession of the Leopard Men approaching the open space before the settlement. Girls and women were dancing, running forward, embracing their men and dressing them with flowers. The children were dancing and flinging flowers and clapping their hands. The men sang and hoisted their spears and an ancient Leopard Man stood before his hut, leaning on his spear and nodding and laughing out of his toothless mouth. The sun was hardly brighter than the occasion. Chimp stole down and round and inserted himself in the tail of the procession behind Beautiful Bird. The leopard hung upside down from four paws and dripped. Beautiful Bird turned, laughing, saw Chimp and embraced him!

"Where was Charging Elephant? We found the trail again! We killed his mighty leopard! We sang round the fireflower but there was no Charging Elephant and no flute! There was a storm of weeping!"

Firefly looked back, as he held his girl in the crook of his arm.

"Where was the Song of the Wind? We lived in a rain-cloud!"

Dragonfly came close, shyly, and put his hand in Chimp's. Chimp burst into tears.

There was a sudden silence. Chimp glanced up through his tears and saw where all were looking. The Namer Of Women, the Woman Namer, She Whose Heart Is Loaded Down With Names was coming across the open space from the Place of Women. She swayed like a palm. White shells clinked delicately on her throat, her ankles, her wrists. Her long, dark hair fell smoothly and modestly over her breasts, her grass skirt rustled. She put one foot behind her, spread her hands on either side. She bent her knees and her head. She straightened up and folded her hands before her. She smiled sweetly.

"Welcome, mighty Leopard Men! What pack, what herd, what pride is swifter, fiercer? And welcome to my Leopard Man, Charging Elephant, who goes to my hut when he wills!"

In his daze, Chimp heard a shout. The Leopard Men were all round him, flowers struck him in the face until Stooping Eagle kissed him.

She spoke again.

"Where have you been, Charging Elephant? The nights have been long and lonely!"

A great delight and strength rose up, up out of his loins. He took the spear from Dragonfly, hoisted it and stamped with his good foot. The song burst out of him.

"I am Water Paw! I am Wounded Leopard!"

Stooping Eagle and Furious Lion were forcing him down. He knelt. The Elder of Elders lifted his spear, then laid it on Chimp's shoulder.

"Water Paw! Wounded Leopard!"

He wept so much, even when he stood up, that he could not see the Namer Of Women but he heard her when she spoke again.

"So go to your secret place, mighty Leopard Men. Take the awful strength of the leopard with you, while we women wonder, and cower; and humbly prepare you a feast of nourishing termite soup, and of dried fish, roots and fruit, and cool, clear water."

"Rah! Rah! Rah!"

So everything ended happily and all changes were for the best. The mountain did not erupt for more than a hundred thousand years; and though the eruption overwhelmed the spa that had grown up round the Hot Springs, by that time there were plenty of people in other places, so it was a small matter.

ENVOY EXTRAORDINARY

1

The Tenth Wonder

The curtains between the loggia and the rest of the villa were no defence against the eunuch's voice. His discourse on passion was understandably but divinely impersonal. It twisted and soared, it punched the third part of a tone suggestive of a whole man's agony, it broke into a controlled wobble, dived, panted neatly in syncopation for breath. The young man who stood against one of the pillars of the loggia continued to roll his head from side to side. There were furrows in his forehead as deep as youth could make them and his eyelids were not screwed up but lowered as if they were a weary and unendurable weight. Beyond and below him the garden was overwhelmed with sunset. A glow, impersonal as the eunuch voice, lay over him, but even so it was possible to see that he was exquisite to look at, tall, red-haired and gentle. His lips fluttered and a sigh came through them.

The old man who sat so restfully by the other pillar of the loggia looked up from his work.

"Mamillius."

Mamillius shrugged inside his toga but did not open his eyes. The old man watched him for a while. The expression on his face was difficult to read, for the sunlight was reflected from the stone pavement and lit him upside down so that the nose was blunted and an artificial benevolence lay about the mouth. There might have been a worried smile under it. He raised his voice a little.

"Let him sing again."

Three notes of a harp, tonic, sub-dominant, dominant, foundations of the universe. The voice rose and the sun continued to sink, with remote and unimpassioned certainty. Mamillius winced, the old man gestured with his left hand and the voice ceased as if he had turned it off.

"Come! Tell me what is the matter."

Mamillius opened his eyes. He turned his head sideways and looked down at the gardens, level after declining level of lawn that yew, cypress and juniper shadowed and formalized, looked listlessly at the last level of all, the glittering sea.

"You would not understand."

The old man crossed his sandalled feet on the footstool and leaned back. He put the tips of his fingers together and an amethyst ring sparkled on one of them. The sunset dyed his toga more gorgeously than the Syrians could manage and the broad, purple fringe looked black.

"Understanding is my business. After all, I am your grandfather, even though you are not from the main trunk of the imperial tree. Tell me what is the matter."

"Time."

The old man nodded gravely.

"Time slips through our fingers like water. We gape in astonishment to see how little is left."

Mamillius had shut his eyes, the furrows were back and he had begun to roll his head against the pillar again.

"Time stands still. There is eternity between a sleep and a sleep. I cannot endure the length of living."

The old man considered for a moment. He put one hand into a basket at his right, took out a paper, glanced at it and threw it into a basket on his left. Much work by many expert hands had gone to giving him the air of clean distinction he cut even before that garden and in that light. He was perfected by art, from the gleaming scalp under the scanty white hair to the tips of the tended toes.

"Millions of people must think that the Emperor's grandson—even one on the left-hand side—is utterly happy."

"I have run through the sources of happiness."

The Emperor made a sudden noise that might have been the beginnings of a shout of laughter if it had not ended in a fit of coughing and a nose-blow in the Roman manner. He turned to his papers again.

"An hour ago you were going to help me with these petitions."

155

"That was before I had begun to read them. Does the whole world think of nothing but cadging favours?"

A nightingale flitted across the garden, came to rest in the dark side of a cypress and tried over a few notes.

"Write some more of your exquisite verses. I particularly liked the ones to be inscribed on an eggshell. They appealed to the gastronome in me."

"I found someone had done it before. I shall not write again."

Then for a while they were silent, prepared to listen to the nightingale: but as if she were conscious of the too-distinguished audience she gave up and flew away.

Mamillius shook out his toga.

"Mourning Itys all these years. What passionate unintelligence!"

"Try the other arts."

"Declamation? Gastronomy?"

"You are too shy for the one and too young for the other."

"I thought you applauded my interest in cooking."

"You talk, Mamillius, but you do not understand. Gastronomy is not the pleasure of youth but the evocation of it."

"The Father of his Country is pleased to be obscure. And I am still bored."

"If you were not so wonderfully transparent I should prescribe senna."

"I am distressingly regular."

"A woman?"

"I hope I am more civilized than that."

This time the Emperor was unable to stop himself. He tried to untwist the laughter out of his face but it convulsed his body instead. He gave up and laughed till the tears jerked out of his eyes. The colour in his grandson's face deepened, caught up the sunset and passed it.

"Am I so funny?"

The Emperor wiped his cheeks.

"I am sorry. I wonder if you will understand that part of my exasperated affection for you is rooted in your very—Mamillius, you are so desperately up-to-date that you dare not enjoy yourself for fear of being thought old-fashioned. If you could only see the world through my regretful and fading eyes!"

"The trouble is, grandfather, I do not even want to. There is nothing new under the sun. Everything has been invented, everything has been written. Time has had a stop."

The Emperor tossed another paper into his basket.

"Have you ever heard of China?"

"No."

"I must have heard of China twenty years ago. An island, I thought, beyond India. Since then, odd fragments of information have filtered through to me. Do you know, Mamillius, China is an Empire bigger than our own?"

"That is nonsense. A contradiction in nature."

"But true, none the less. I sometimes fall into a daze of wonder as I imagine this ball of earth held, as it were, in

157

two hands—one light brown and the other, according to my information, jaundice yellow. Perhaps at last man will be confronted with his long-lost twin as in that comedy."

"Travellers' tales."

"I try to prove to you how vast and wonderful life is."

"Do you suggest that I should go exploring?"

"You could not go by sea and it would take ten years by track or river if the Arimaspians would let you. Stay home and amuse an old man who grows lonely."

"Thank you for allowing me to be your fool."

"Boy," said the Emperor strongly, "go and get mixed up in a good bloody battle."

"I leave that sort of thing to your official heir. Posthumus is an insensitive bruiser. He can have all the battles he wants. Besides, a battle cheapens life and I find life cheap enough already."

"Then the Father of his Country can do nothing for his own grandson."

"I am tired of twiddling my fingers."

The Emperor looked at him more closely than the remark seemed to warrant. "Have I been very foolish? Be careful, Mamillius. A condition of our unusual friendship is that you keep your fingers out of hot water. Go on twiddling them. I want you to have that long life even if in the end you die of boredom. Do not become ambitious."

"I am not ambitious for power."

"Continue to convince Posthumus of that. Leave ruling to him. He likes it."

Mamillius looked at the curtains, took a step forward and murmured to the Emperor.

"Yet you would prefer that I should inherit the purple fringe on your toga!"

The Emperor leaned forward and answered him urgently.

"If his agents heard you we should neither of us live a year. Never say such a thing again. It is an order."

Mamillius returned to his pillar, while the Emperor took up another paper, held it in the sunset-glow and tossed it aside. For a time there was silence between them. The nightingale, assured of darkness and privacy, returned to the cypress and her song. The Emperor spoke softly at last.

"Go down the steps, cross the lawn that fills this coombe so neatly, pick your way past the lily-pond and enter the cliff-tunnel. After a hundred paces you will stand on the harbour quay———"

"I know the neighbourhood well enough."

"You will not be able to see much by the time you get there; but say to yourself, 'Here, shielded from the sea by the two quays are a hundred ships, a thousand houses, ten thousand people. And every one would give his ears to be the bastard but favourite grandson of the Emperor'."

"Warehouses, taverns, brothels. Tar, oil, bilges, dung, sweat."

"You dislike humanity."

"And you?"

"I accept it."

"I avoid it."

"We must get Posthumus to allow you a governorship. Egypt?"

"Greece, if I must."

"Booked, I am afraid," said the Emperor regretfully. "There is even a waiting list."

"Egypt, then."

"A part of Egypt. If you go, Mamillius, it will be for your own sake. You would find nothing of me on your return but ashes and a monument or two. Be happy then, if only to cheer an ageing civil servant."

"What has Egypt to make me happy? There is nothing new, even out of Africa."

The Emperor unrolled another paper, glanced at it, smiled, then allowed himself to laugh.

"Here is something new for you. They are two of your prospective subjects. You had better see them."

Listlessly Mamillius accepted the paper, stood with his back to the Emperor and held it up to the light. He let go the end and glanced over his shoulder, grinning, as the paper rolled itself up. He turned and they laughed in each other's eyes. The Emperor laughed, enjoying himself, younger, delighted. Mamillius was suddenly younger, his laugh uncertain in pitch.

"He wants to play boats with Caesar."

So they laughed together under the song of the nightingale. The Emperor was the first to compose himself to stillness. He nodded towards the curtains. Mamillius went towards them, pulled one aside and spoke in a coldly formal voice.

"The Emperor will see the petitioners Phanocles and Euphrosyne."

Then he was back by the pillar and they were nodding and grinning at each other conspiratorially.

But Caesar could not be approached as though he were no more than a man. A fat secretary came through the curtains, sank on one knee and rested the tablets on the other. With a stamp and clank a soldier in full armour marched into the loggia. He came to attention behind the Emperor and a little to one side, rasped out a sword and flashed it upright. There were voices whispering behind the curtain and two slaves drew them back. Someone struck a staff on stone paving.

"The Emperor permits you to approach him."

A man came through the curtain and a woman followed him carrying a burden. The slaves dropped the curtain and the man stood for a moment, perhaps dazzled by the sunset so that they had a moment or two to inspect him. He wore a light-coloured tunic and over that a long green cloak. His dark hair and beard were wild, ruffled either by the wind of his own approach or by some exterior insolence of weather that was not permitted to invade the Emperor's seclusion. The cloak was threadbare, patched and dusty. No one had taken care of his hands and feet. His face was lumpy, haphazard and to be accepted as nothing more than the front of a head.

The woman who had followed him shrank aside to the shadowy corner that seemed her natural place. She was little but a pillar of drapery, for a veil was over her head and caught loosely across her face. She stood sideways to the men and bowed her head over the bundle she carried. The instep lifted the long robe so that it revealed a sandal and four inches of modelled foot. The soldier made no sign behind his sword: only his eyes swivelling sideways raked her, assessing, expertly removing the wrappings, judging with the intuitive skill of long practice, from the few hints she allowed him, the woman who lay beneath. He saw a hand half-hidden, the rounded shape of a knee beneath the fabric. His eyes returned to their divided stare on either side of the sword. His lips pursed and rounded. Breathed through at a more propitious time and place they would have whistled.

Suspecting this transaction, the Emperor glanced quickly behind him. The soldier's eyes stared straight ahead. It was impossible to believe that they had ever moved or would ever move again. The Emperor glanced at Mamillius.

He was watching the woman sideways, his eyes, swivelling, raked her, removing the wrappings, judging with the intuitive and boundless optimism of youth the woman who lay beneath.

The Emperor leaned back happily. The man found his woman and took the bundle from her but could see nowhere to put it. He peered short-sightedly at the Emperor's footstool. The Emperor crooked a finger at the secretary.

"Take a note."

He watched Mamillius, kindly, triumphantly.

"Pyrrha's Pebbles, Jehovah's Spontaneous Creation, or the Red Clay of Thoth: but it has always appeared to me that some god found man on all fours, put a knee in the small of his back and jerked him upright. The sensualist relies on this. The wise man remembers it."

But Mamillius was not listening.

The wild man made up his mind. He removed some sacking from the bundle, bent and placed a model ship on the pavement between the Emperor and Mamillius. She was about a yard long and unhandsome. The Emperor glanced from her to the man.

"You are Phanocles?"

"Phanocles, Caesar, the son of Myron, an Alexandrian."

"Myron? You are librarian."

"I was, Caesar—an assistant—until——"

He gestured with extraordinary violence towards the boat. The Emperor continued to look at him.

"And you want to play boats with Caesar?"

He was able to keep the amusement out of his face but it crept into his voice. Phanocles turned in desperation to Mamillius but he was still occupied and more frankly now. Suddenly Phanocles burst into a flood of speech.

"There was obstruction, Caesar, from top to bottom. I

163

was wasting my time, they said, and I was dabbling, in black magic, they said, and they laughed. I am a poor man and when the last of my father's money—he left me a little you understand—not much—and I spent that—what are we to do, Caesar?"

The Emperor watched him, saying nothing. He could see that Phanocles had not been blinded by the sunset. The dregs of it were enough to show him that the man was short-sighted. The frustration of this gave him an air of bewilderment and anger as if some perpetual source of astonishment and outrage hung in the empty air a yard before his face.

"—and I knew if I could only reach Caesar——"

But there had been obstruction and more obstruction, mockery, incomprehension, anger, persecution.

"How much did it cost you to see me today?"

"Seven pieces of gold."

"That seems reasonable. I am not in Rome."

"It was all I had."

"Mamillius. See that Phanocles does not lose by his visit. Mamillius!"

"Caesar."

Shadows were creeping down from the roof of the loggia and welling out of the corners. The nightingale still sang from the tall cypress. The Emperor's eyes went like the soldier's to the veiled women then, unlike his, to Mamillius.

"And your sister?"

"Euphrosyne, Caesar, a free woman and a virgin."

164

The Emperor allowed his palm to turn and his finger to crook until there lay on his lap the image of a beckoning hand. Drawn by that irresistible compulsion Euphrosyne moved noiselessly out of her corner and stood before him. The folds of her dress rearranged themselves, the veil fluttered over her mouth.

The Emperor glanced at Mamillius and said to himself:

"There is nothing new under the sun."

He turned to Euphrosyne.

"Lady, let us see your face."

Phanocles took a sudden step forward and found himself checked by the model.

He danced to save it from injury.

"Caesar——"

"You must accustom yourselves to our Western manners."

He glanced down at the sandalled toes, the moulded knee, up at the unbelievable hands clutched so tightly into the fabric of her dress. He nodded gently and put out the hand with the amethyst on it in assurance.

"We intend no discourtesy, lady. Modesty is the proper ornament of virginity. But let us see your eyes at least so that we may know to whom we speak."

Her head turned in the veil to her brother, but he was standing helplessly, hands clasped and mouth open. At last one hand drew down over her breast a little way and the veil came too so that it revealed the upper part of her face. She looked at the Emperor and then her head sank as though her whole body were a poppy stem and hardly strong enough for the weight.

The Emperor looked back at her eyes, smiling and frowning. He said nothing, but the unspoken news of his need had gone forth. The curtains parted and three women paced solemnly on to the loggia. Each seemed to carry a double handful of light in cupped hands so that faces were lit and the fingers a rose-coloured transparency. The Emperor, still watching Euphrosyne, began to arrange these nameless lamps with movements of a finger. One he beckoned to the right of her and forward, one behind her so that immediately the light ran and glittered in her hair. The third he moved in, close, close, bade the light rise till it was lifted by her face on the left side, so near that its warmth fluttered a curl by her ear.

The Emperor turned to Mamillius, who said nothing. There was a shocked look on his face as though he had been jerked out of a deep sleep. With a sudden motion Euphrosyne covered her face again and it was as though a fourth light had been extinguished. The soldier's sword was shaking.

The Emperor leaned back in his chair and spoke to Phanocles.

"You bring the tenth wonder of the world with you."

The sweat was running down Phanocles' face. He looked at the model in bewildered relief.

"But I have not explained, Caesar——"

The Emperor waved his hand.

166

"Calm yourself. No harm is intended to you or your sister. Mamillius, they are our guests."

Mamillius let out his breath and looked at the Emperor. His head began to turn from side to side restlessly as though he were trying to break loose from invisible strings. Yet the Emperor's announcement had set another pattern in motion. The women ranged themselves to light the curtained doorway and the grave house dame came through it, willing to give of her plenteous store. She inclined her head to the Emperor, to Mamillius, to Euphrosyne, took her by the wrist and led her away. The curtains dropped together and the loggia was dark at last, the brightest lights were where the fishing boats danced by their nets. Mamillius came close to Phanocles and spoke to him in a voice that remembered how recently it had broken.

"What is her voice like? How does she speak?"

"She speaks very seldom, lord. I cannot remember the quality of her voice."

"Men have built temples for objects of less beauty."

"She is my sister!"

The Emperor stirred in his chair.

"If you are so poor, Phanocles, has it never occurred to you to make your fortune by a brilliant connection?"

Phanocles peered wildly round the loggia as though he were trapped.

"What woman would you have me marry, Caesar?"

Into the incredulous silence that followed his speech the nightingale spilled a rill of song. She had evoked the evening star that sparkled now in a patch of dense blue between the blacknesses of the junipers. Mamillius spoke in his rebroken voice.

"Has she an ambition, Phanocles?"

The Emperor laughed a little.

"A beautiful woman is her own ambition."

"She is all the reasons in the world for poetry."

"Corinthian is your style, Mamillius. However—continue."

"She is of epic simplicity."

"Your eternities of boredom will be sufficient for all twenty-four books."

"Don't laugh at me."

"I am not laughing. You have made me very happy. Phanocles—how did you preserve this phœnix?"

Phanocles was groping in a double darkness.

"What am I to say, Caesar? She is my sister. Her beauty has come up, as it were, overnight."

He paused, searching for words. They burst out of him.

"I do not understand you or any man. Why can they not let us be? Of what importance is the bedding of individuals? When there is such an ocean at our feet of eternal relationships to examine or confirm?"

They heard in the darkness a clucking sound from Phanocles' throat as though he were about to be sick. But when he spoke, the words were at once ordered and pointless.

"If you let a stone drop from your hand it will fall."

The Emperor's chair creaked.

"I hope we are following you."

"Each substance has affinities of an eternal and immutable nature with every other substance. A man who understands them—this lord here——"

"My grandson, the Lord Mamillius."

"Lord, do you know much of law?"

"I am a Roman."

Mamillius felt the wind of arms flung wide. He peered into the darkness of the loggia and made out a dark gesticulating shape.

"There then! You can move easily in the world of law. I can move in the world of substance and force because I credit the universe with at least a lawyer's intelligence. Just as you, who know the law, could have your way with me since I do not, so I can have my way with the universe."

"Confused," said the Emperor. "Illogical and extremely hubristic. Tell me, Phanocles. When you talk like this do people ever tell you you are mad?"

Phanocles' bewildered face swam forward in the gloom. He sensed the model and hoped to avoid it. Then there was something before his face—a sword blade that glistened dully. He backed clumsily away.

The Emperor repeated the words as though he had not said them before.

"—tell you you are mad?"

"Yes, Caesar. That is why I—severed my connection with the library."

169

"I understand."

"Am I mad?"

"Let us hear further."

"The universe is a machine."

Mamillius stirred.

"Are you a magician?"

"There is no magic."

"Your sister is a living proof and epitome of magic."

"Then she is beyond Nature's legislation."

"That may well be. Is there any poetry in your universe?"

Phanocles turned, tormented, to the Emperor.

"That is how they all talk, Caesar. Poetry, magic, religion——"

The Emperor chuckled.

"Be careful, Greek. You are talking to the Pontifex Maximus."

Phanocles darted the shadow of a finger at his face.

"Does Caesar believe in the things that the Pontifex Maximus has to do?"

"I prefer not to answer that question."

"Lord Mamillius. Do you believe in your very heart that there is an unreasonable and unpredictable force of poetry outside your rolls of paper?"

"How dull your life must be!"

"Dull?"

He took a half-step towards the Emperor, remembered the sword and stopped in time.

"My life is passed in a condition of ravished astonishment."

The Emperor answered him patiently.

"Then a mere Emperor can do nothing for you. Diogenes was no happier than you in his tub. All I can do is to stand out of the sun."

"Yet I am destitute. Without your help I must starve. With it I can change the universe."

"Will you improve it?"

"He is mad, Caesar."

"Let him be, Mamillius. Phanocles, in my experience, changes are almost always for the worse. Yet I entertain you for my—for your sister's sake. Be brief. What do you want?"

There had been obstruction. The ship, not his sister, was the tenth wonder; he could not understand men, but with this ship the Emperor would be more famous than Alexander. Mamillius had ceased to listen and was muttering to himself, and beating time with his finger.

The Emperor said nothing as Phanocles rambled on, did nothing, but allowed a little cold air to form round him in the darkness and extend outwards. At last for all the man's insensitivity he faltered to a stop.

Mamillius spoke.

" 'The speechless eloquence of beauty——' "

"I have heard that before somewhere," said the Emperor thoughtfully. "Bion, I think, or is it Meleager?"

Phanocles cried out.

"Caesar!"

"Ah, yes. Your model. What do you want?"

"Let a light be brought."

One of the women returned with the ritual solemnity to the loggia.

"What is you model called?"

"She has no name."

"A ship without a name? Find one, Mamillius."

"I do not care for her. *Amphitrite*."

Mamillius yawned elaborately.

"I think, Grandfather, with your permission——"

The Emperor beamed up at him. "Ensure that our guests are comfortable."

Mamillius moved with a rush towards the curtain.

"Mamillius!"

"Caesar?"

"I am sorry that you are so bored."

Mamillius paused.

"Bored? Yes. I am. Sleep well, Grandfather."

Mamillius strolled through the curtains with an air of leisurely indifference.

They heard how his steps quickened immediately he was out of sight. The Emperor laughed and looked down at the boat.

"She is unseaworthy, flat-bottomed, with little sheer and bows like a corn-barge. What are the ornaments? Have they a religious significance?"

"Hardly, Caesar."

"So you want to play boats with me? If I were not charmed with your innocence I should be displeased at your presumption."

"I have three toys for you, Caesar. This is only the first."

"I entertain you."

"Caesar. Have you ever seen water boiling in a pot?"

"I have."

"There is much steam evolved which escapes into the air. If the pot were closed what would happen?"

"The steam could not escape."

"The pot would burst. The force exerted by steam is titanic."

"Really!" said the Emperor with interest. "Have you ever seen a pot burst?"

Phanocles mastered himself.

"Beyond Syria there is a savage tribe. They inhabit a land full of natural oil and inflammable vapour. When they desire to cook they lead the vapour through pipes into stoves at the sides of their houses. The meat these natives eat is tough and must be cooked for a long time. They put one dish on top of another, inverted. Now the steam builds up a pressure under the pot that penetrates the meat and cooks it thoroughly and quickly."

"Will not the steam burst the pot?"

"There is the ingenuity of the device. If the pressure becomes too great it will lift the pot and allow the steam to escape. But do you not see? The upper lid is lifted—steam could lift a weight that an elephant would baulk at."

173

The Emperor was sitting upright, leaning forward, his hands on the arms of his chair.

"And the flavour, Phanocles! It will be confined! The whole wonderful intention of the comestible will be preserved by magic!"

He stood up and began to pace round the loggia.

"We should taste meat for the first time——"

"But——"

"I have always been a primitive where meat is concerned. Elephant's foot and mammoth, your rarities, spices, unguents, they are unworthy and vulgar. My grandson would plead that we should explore all variables and enlarge, as it were, the frontiers of gustatory experience——"

"My ship——"

"——but that is boy's talk. To taste meat in its exquisite simplicity would be a return to those experiences of youth that time has blunted. There should be a wood fire, a healthy tiredness in the limbs, and if possible a sense of peril. Then a robust red wine——"

They faced each other, two mouths open but for different reasons.

"Phanocles, we are on the verge of an immense discovery. What do the natives call their two dishes?"

"A pressure cooker."

"How soon could you make me one? Or perhaps if we simply inverted one dish over another——"

He was tapping one finger into the palm of the other

174

hand, looking sideways at the garden but not seeing it.

"—or fish perhaps? Fowl? I think on the whole that fish would be preferable. One must find a little white wine of sufficient modesty to disclaim any self-pretension and sink itself wholly. Trout? Turbot? And at the same time of sufficient integrity to wait devotedly in attendance——"

He turned back to Phanocles.

"There is a southern vintage from that place in Sicily if I could remember the name——"

"Caesar!"

"You must dine with me now and we will formulate a plan of action. Yes, I dine very late. I find it gives me an appetite."

"But my boat, Caesar!"

"*Amphitrite?*"

Poised, ready to go, the Emperor waited.

"I could give you anything, Phanocles. What do you want?"

"When the wind falls what happens to a ship?"

Indulgently, the Emperor turned to him.

"She waits for the next one. The master invokes a wind. Sacrifices and so on."

"But if he does not believe in a wind god?"

"Then I suppose he does not get a wind."

"But if the wind fails at a moment of crisis for your warships?"

"The slaves row."

"And when they tire?"

"They are beaten."

"But if they become so tired that beating is useless?"

"Then they are thrown overboard. You have the Socratic method."

Phanocles allowed his hands to drop to his side in a gesture of defeat. The Emperor smiled consolingly at him.

"You are tired and hungry. Have no fear for yourself or your sister. You have become very precious to me and your sister shall be my ward."

"I do not think of her."

The Emperor was puzzled.

"What do you want then?"

"I have tried to say. I want to build you a warship after the pattern of *Amphitrite*."

"A warship is a serious undertaking. I cannot treat you as though you were a qualified shipwright when you are only an ex-librarian."

"Then give me a hull—any hull. Give me an old cornbarge if you will, and sufficient money to convert her after this fashion."

"Of course, my dear Phanocles, anything you like. I will give the necessary orders."

"And my other inventions?"

"The pressure cooker?"

"No. The next one. I call it an explosive."

"Something that claps out? How strange! What is the third invention?"

"I will keep it in reserve to surprise you."

The Emperor nodded in relief.

"Do so. Make your ship and your clapper-outer. But first—the pressure cooker." Beaming, he reached out his hand, laid it gently on Phanocles' arm, turned him without force. And, compelled to follow by the first stirrings of courtiership, Phanocles kept in step, bowing a little towards the Emperor. The curtains swung open, released a flood of light that received and hid them. The light lay uninterruptedly on the secretary, the soldier, the empty chair; gleamed brightly from *Amphitrite's* brass boiler and funnel.

2

Talos

Mamillius stepped down from the loggia to the garden. He was pleased with his appearance. The wide straw hat, enabling one to stand or walk in a pool of shade, was sufficiently un-Roman to be a declaration of independence without being openly defiant. The light cloak, attached to either shoulder and cut from the thinnest Egyptian linen, added masculine dignity without oppression. If one walked fast—and for a moment he did so quite deliberately—it floated on the air and gave an effect of mercurial speed. The tunic was daringly short and slit at the sides but this, after all, was merely fashionable. If I were to come on her now, he thought, sitting between the lichened Naiads, would she not draw the veil from her face and speak? He kept his eyes open for her as he passed down the many steps, but the hot gardens were deserted. Each square of lawn was like velvet as it should have been according to literary convention and the clipped yew patterns were less alive than the statuary they surrounded. He peered into arbours and herb gardens, threaded his way between groups of stone Hamadryads, Fauns, Bronze Boys; he made the usual salutation mechanically before the Herms that stood among the denser thickets.

But the trouble was she would not speak and was rarely to be seen. I know a little about love now, he thought, and not only from reading about it. Love is this nagging preoccupation, this feeling that the treasure of life has condensed itself to the little space wherever she is. I guess ahead and understand that love was reared in the wilderness and sucked the lion's dug. What does she think of me, how does she speak, is she in love?

A kind of burning spread over him and set his flesh trembling. I dislike this, he thought, I must not think of her. At that, a procession of horribly masculine lovers presented themselves to his imagination. By the time he had reached the lily-pond on the edge of the cliff at the foot of the garden he was struggling up out of his mind like a diver coming out of deep water.

"I wish I were bored again."

Perhaps the hat had not been such a good idea after all. The edges of his private pool of shadow were dulled and though the heat was already intense the sky to seaward was not as blue as it had been yesterday. There was a faint haze lying along the horizon and spreading towards the land. He spoke to a weather-beaten Satyr.

"We shall have thunder."

The Satyr continued to grin toothily. He knew what it was all about. Euphrosyne. Mamillius jerked himself away and turned to the left where the tunnel ran through the little headland and down to the harbour in the next cove. The sentry at the mouth of the tunnel came to attention. Partly because of the uninviting tunnel and partly because talking to soldiers always gave him a comfortable feeling of superiority, Mamillius spoke to him.

"Good morning. Are you comfortable here?"

"Sir."

"How many of you are there?"

"Twenty-five, sir. Five officers and twenty men, sir."

"Where are you billeted?"

The soldier jerked his head.

"Through the tunnel, sir. In the trireme alongside the quay."

"So I shall have to climb across her if I want to visit the new ship?"

"Sir."

"Tiresome. Pleasanter in the Emperor's garden than in the harbour, isn't it?"

The soldier thought.

"Quieter, sir. Very nice for them as likes a bit of quiet."

"You prefer your billets in hell?"

"Sir?"

Mamillius turned away and walked into the dark tunnel and a confusion of green after-images that remembered the toothy Satyr. He held his breath for as long as possible because the guards used the tunnel as more than an approach to the gardens. The after-images were pierced and then replaced by his first view of hell.

To anyone but an Emperor's grandson in a brief and slit tunic, hell would have seemed an interesting and even attractive place. The port was built in a small bay that was like half a cup. Round it climbed gaudy warehouses and tenements that were painted red and yellow and white. The inside of the cup had a half-circle of quay running round it where every kind of vessel was lying, five or ten deep. The entrance to the cup was defended from the sea by two quays that almost met each other. The tunnel emerged on to the root of the nearer quay. Tenements, quays, warehouses, ships—they crawled with people. There were seamen, slaves or free, swinging over the sides of ships, and smearing on tar or paint. There were boys swung aloft and working at running rigging, there were men in skiffs and barges, and naked harbour rats oaring themselves after driftwood through the lolloping garbage. The hot air of the harbour shook the warehouses and tenements, shook the steep hills, would probably have shaken the sky if there had been any clouds to reveal the movement. Smoke from caulking braziers, from steaming pipes where the planks were twisted, from vats and cookshops and galleys dirtied the air and cast a hundred brazen shadows. The sun burned into all this and blazed from the water in the middle of the harbour in molten shapelessness.

181

Mamillius pulled down the brim of his straw hat and folded a corner of cloak across his nose. He paused for a while, appalled and secretly gratified by his genuine distaste for humanity and the violent mess they made of themselves. Moreover he felt he had a contribution to make to the mythology of hell. It not only stank and burned; it roared. Noise climbed with the heat, vibration, a drum-roll of sound on which screams floated like the twisted flight of a gull.

He turned from the port itself to the quay where his business was. The quay stretched across half the port to the entrance with a shoulder-high wall to seaward. There were three ships made fast to it. The first, on his left hand and only a few yards from him, was the imperial barge. She lay low in the water, her rowers sleeping on their benches in the sun, a slave boy doing something to the cushions of her throne under its huge purple baldachino. Ahead of her was the slim shape of the trireme, her oars unshipped and stowed. Slaves were working on her deck, but she was very dirty from the traffic that crossed and re-crossed her, for *Amphitrite* was made fast on the outboard side of her, squat and uniquely ugly.

Mamillius strolled along the quay as slowly as possible, putting off the moment when he would have to endure the heat from her hold. He stopped by Phanocles' second invention and examined it curiously, for he had not seen it before. The tormentum had been set up and trained over the wall, pointing out to sea. Against all military sense, Phanocles had wound back the chain that served for a string and cocked the mechanism. Even the sledge that would drive the peg and release the string was lying ready. There was a bolt lying in the groove and on the other end of the bolt was a shining keg ending in a brass butterfly with a projecting iron sting. The thing was a suitable insect for hell. Strike the peg and the bolt would buzz seaward, out to the fishing boats, would bear the keg to them, a drink with the Emperor's compliments.

Mamillius shuddered at the machine, then laughed as he remembered Phanocles' explanation. In the end, desperately, as though the Emperor were a child, he had flung out his arms, said one sentence and refused to add to it.

"I have shut lightning in the key and can release it when I will."

The sentry who had been dozing behind the tormentum found himself discovered and attempted to cover his fault by chatting as though he and Mamillius were on one side of a fence and military discipline on the other.

"Nice little horror, isn't she, sir?"

Mamillius nodded without speaking. The sentry looked up at the heat haze creeping over the quay wall.

"Going to have thunder, sir."

Mamillius made the sign that averts evil and walked hastily along the quay. There was no sentry on the trireme to meet him and no one to greet him at the gangway. Now that he was aboard her he could identify the ground bass to the uproar of the harbour—the slaves in every ship were growling like beasts that lust for the food of the arena. The only silent slaves were those working listlessly, moodily on deck. He crossed the trireme amidships and stood looking down at *Amphitrite*.

She made the tormentum look like a toy. Projecting from her on either side were the biggest wheels in the world and each wheel bore a dozen paddles, A great bar of iron that Phanocles had had twisted into a wicked shape writhed its way across the deck between them. Four metal hands held this bar, two pushing, two pulling back. Behind the hands were iron forearms and upper arms that slid back into sleeves of brass. Mamillius knew what Phanocles called the sleeves. They were the pistons; and because there was no other way of making them with the ludicrous accuracy he demanded they had been drawn off two alabaster pillars that had been intended for a temple of the Graces.

Reminded by the Graces of Euphrosyne, Mamillius turned aft. Between the pistons was the most daunting thing of all: Talos, the man of brass. He was headless, a flashing sphere half-sunk in the deck, his four arms reached forward and gripped the wicked crank. Between him and the crank, fitting in the space that the arms left between them, was a brass funnel, tall as a mast, scandalous parody of the Holy Phallus.

There were few men about. A slave was doing something highly technical to one of the steering paddles and someone was shovelling coal in the hold. The coal grit lay everywhere on her deck and sides and paddles. Only Talos was clean, waist deep in the deck, breathing steam, heat, and glistening with oil. Once *Amphitrite* had been a corn-barge that labourers had hauled up the river to Rome, an ungainly box, smelling of chaff and old wood, comfortable and harmless. But now she was possessed. Talos sat in her, the insect pointed over the harbour wall and hell roared.

Phanocles poked his head out of the hold. He squinted at Mamillius through his sweat, shook his beard and wiped his face with a piece of waste.

"We are almost ready."

"You know the Emperor is coming?"

Phanocles nodded. Mamillius grimaced at the coal dust.

"Haven't you made any preparations for him?"

"He said there was to be no ceremony."

"But *Amphitrite* is filthily dirty!"

Phanocles peered down at the deck.

"This coal costs a fortune."

Mamillius stepped aboard gingerly.

"The hottest corner in hell."

The heat hit him from the boiler and sweat streamed down his face. Phanocles looked round at Talos for a moment then handed Mamillius the piece of waste. He conceded the point.

"I suppose it is hotter than usual."

Mamillius waved away the waste and wiped his streaming face on the corner of his elegant cloak. Now that he was cheek by jowl with Talos he could see more of his construction. Just above deck level at the after-end of the sphere was a projection surrounded with springs. Phanocles, following his gaze, reached out and flicked the brass with his fingers so that it tinged and gave out a puff of steam. He looked moodily at the projection.

"See that? I call it a safety valve, I gave exact instructions——"

But the craftsman had added a winged Boreas who touched the brass with an accidental toe and rounded his cheeks to eject a fair wind. Mamillius smiled with constraint.

"Very pretty."

The springs strained, steam shot out and Mamillius leapt back. Phanocles rubbed his hands.

"Now we are ready."

He came sweatily close to Mamillius.

"I have had her out in the centre of the harbour and once out in the bay. She works as certainly and easily as the stars."

Mamillius, averting his face, found himself regarding his own distorted face in Talos' shining side. It faded away from the mouth and pointed nose. No matter how he moved it followed him with the incurious but remorseless stare of a fish. The heat from the boiler and the smoking funnel was like a blow.

"I want to get out of this——"

He made his way under the contorted cranks and paused in the bows. The air was a little cooler here so that he took off his straw hat and fanned himself with it. Phanocles walked forward too and they leaned their backs against the bulwarks. Slaves were working on the fo'castle of the trireme only a few feet above them.

"This is an evil ship."

Phanocles finished wiping his hands and dropped the waste over the side. They turned to watch it drift. Phanocles pointed upward with his thumb.

"She is not evil. Only useful. Would you sooner do that?"

Mamillius glanced up at the slaves. They were clustered round the metal crab and, he could see most of it though the claws were hidden by the trireme's deck.

"I don't understand you."

"Presently they will centre the yard-arm and swing the crab up—all ten tons of it. Steam would do it for them without fuss or exertion."

"I do not have to swing the crab up. I am not a slave."

They were silent for a while, standing on tip-toe to inspect the crab. It was a spreadeagled mass of lead and iron, its claws resting on blocks of stone to keep them from cutting through the deck. It was as strictly utilitarian a mass as could have been found anywhere in the Empire, for its sole use was to be dropped through an enemy's bilges and sink her outright: but the same impulse that had made the brass on the keg into a butterfly and stood a Boreas on the safety valve had been at work on the crab too. The makers had indicated the eyes and the joints of the legs. It had a kind of formal significance and the slaves were tending it—cleaning the claws—as if it were more than metal. Other slaves were swinging the seventy-foot yard round, were centring the hoist over the ring.

Mamillius turned and looked along *Amphitrite*'s deck.

"Life is a perplexing muddle, Phanocles."

"I shall clean it up."

"Meanwhile you are making it dirtier."

"No slaves, no armies."

"What is wrong with slaves and armies? You might as well say, 'No eating or drinking or making love'."

For a while again they were silent, listening to the roar of the port and the shouted orders from the trireme.

"Ease her down. Handsomely!"

"This evening the Emperor is going to try your pressure cooker. The one you made for him."

"He will forget all that when he tries *Amphitrite*."

Mamillius squinted up at the sun. It was not so bright, but he still fanned himself.

"Lord Mamillius—has he forgiven us for the improvised cooker?"

"I think so."

"Sway back. Take the strain. Walk. One, two. One, two."

"And, after all, without that experiment I should have never known that a safety valve was necessary."

"He said that a mammoth was too much to begin with. Blamed me."

"Still?"

Mamillius shook his head.

"All the same, he is sorry about the three cooks and the north wing of the villa."

Phanocles nodded, sweating. He frowned at a memory.

"Do you think that was what he meant by a 'Sense if possible of peril'?"

The slave who had been firing the furnace climbed to the deck and they watched him idly. He threw a bucket over the side on a rope's end, hauled up water and tipped it over his naked body. The water flowed along the deck, carrying snakes of coal dust. Again and again he laved the filthy harbour water over himself. Phanocles called to him.

"Clean the deck here."

The slave touched his smeared forelock. He drew up another bucketful, then shot it along the deck so that water splashed over their feet. They started up with a shout of annoyance and there came the sound of a rope breaking under strain. *Amphitrite* ducked under them, sidled and made a loud wooden remark as though she had crunched one of her own timbers with metal teeth. There came a dull thump from the harbour bottom, then a huge cascade of water fell on them from the sky, water full of garbage and mud and oil and tar. Phanocles stumbled forward and Mamillius bowed under the torrent, too shocked even to curse. The water ceased to fall from the sky but surged, waist-deep, over the decks instead. Puffs of steam spurted from Talos like ejaculations of rage. Then the water had all streamed away, the decks were shining and the roar of the harbour had risen to a frenzy. Mamillius was cursing at last under a hat like a cow pat and in clothes that clung greasily to him. Then he was silent, turning to the place where they had leaned and talked. The crab had snatched away six feet of the bulwarks, had torn off planking from the deck and laid bare the splintered beam ends. The huge cable led straight down from the yard of the trireme into the water where yellow mud still stank and swirled. A mob of men were brawling on the trireme, and soldiers were among them, using the pommels of their swords. A man broke free. He stumbled to the quay, seized a loose stone, clasped it to his stomach and plunged over the harbour wall into the sea. The struggle sorted itself out. Two of the Emperor's guards were bashing heads impartially.

Mamillius went white slowly under the filth that covered him.

"That is the first time anyone has tried to kill me."

Phanocles was gaping at the broken bulwarks. Mamillius began to shiver.

"I have harmed no one."

The captain of the trireme came, leaping nimbly to the deck.

"Lord, what can I say?"

The frenzy from the harbour seemed as though it would never die away. There was the sense of eyes, thousands of eyes watching across the deceptive embroidery of the water. Mamillius gazed wildly round into the white air. His nerves were jerking. Phanocles spoke in a foolishly complaining voice.

"They have damaged her."

"Curse your filthy ship——"

"Lord. The slave who cut the cable has drowned himself. We are trying to find the ringleader."

Mamillius cried out.

"Oloito!"

Use of a literary word was a safety valve. He shivered no more but began to weep instead. Phanocles put his shaking hands close to his face and examined them as though they might have information of value.

"Accidents happen. Only the other day a plank missed me by inches. We are still alive."

The captain saluted.

"With your permission, lord."

He leapt back aboard the trireme. Mamillius turned a streaming face to Phanocles.

"Why have I enemies? I wish I were dead."

All at once it seemed to him that nothing was safe or certain but the mysterious beauty of Euphrosyne.

"Phanocles—give me your sister."

Phanocles took his hands from his face.

"We are free people, lord."

"I mean, to marry her."

Phanocles cried out in his thick voice.

"This is too much! A plank, a crab—and now this——!"

Hell closed in on Mamillius, haze-white and roaring. Somewhere in the sky the thunder grumbled.

"I cannot bear life without her."

Phanocles muttered, his eyes on Talos.

"You have not even seen her face. And you are grandson to the Emperor."

"He will do anything I want."

Phanocles glanced sideways at him, savagely.

"How old are you, lord? Is it eighteen or seventeen?"

"I am a man."

Phanocles made a pattern of his face that was intended for a sneer.

"Officially."

Mamillius set his teeth.

"I am sorry for my tears. I have been shaken."

He hiccuped loudly.

"Am I forgiven?"

Phanocles looked him over.

"What do you want with my forgiveness?"

"Euphrosyne."

All at once Mamillius was trembling again. Beautiful shoots of life sprouted in him. But Phanocles was frowning.

"I cannot, explain, lord."

"Say no more now. We shall speak to the Emperor. He will persuade you."

There came the crash of a salute from the mouth of the tunnel.

The Emperor was walking briskly for his age. His crier went before him.

"Way for the Emperor!"

There was a guard and several veiled women with him. Mamillius began to rush round the deck in a panic, but the women detached themselves from the group of men and ranged themselves by the harbour wall. Phanocles shaded his eyes.

"He has brought her to watch the demonstration."

The captain of the trireme was hurrying along by the Emperor, explaining as he went, and the Emperor was nodding his silver head pensively. He mounted the gangway to the trireme, crossed her deck and looked down at the strange ship before him. Even in these surroundings his spare figure in the white, purple-fringed toga cut a shape of clean distinction. He declined a helping hand and stepped down to *Amphitrite*'s deck.

"Don't try to tell me about the crab, Mamillius. The captain has told me all about it. I congratulate you on your escape. You too, Phanocles, of course. We shall have to abandon the demonstration."

"Caesar!"

"You see, Phanocles, I shall not be at the villa this evening. I will examine your pressure cooker another time."

Phanocles' mouth was open again.

"In fact," said the Emperor agreeably, "we shall be at sea in *Amphitrite*."

"Caesar."

"Stay with me, Mamillius. I have news for you."

He paused and cocked his ear critically at the harbour noises.

"I am not popular."

Mamillius shook again.

"Neither am I. They tried to kill me."

The Emperor smiled grimly.

"It was not the slaves, Mamillius. I have received a report from Illyria."

A look of appalled understanding appeared beneath the mud on Mamillus' face.

"Posthumus?"

"He has broken off his campaign. He has concentrated his army on the seaport and is stripping the coast of every ship from triremes to fishing boats."

Mamillius made a quick and aimless step that nearly took him into the arms of Talos.

"He is tired of heroics."

The Emperor came close and laid a finger delicately on his grandson's sodden tunic.

"No, Mamillius. He has heard that the Emperor's grandson is becoming interested in ships and weapons of war. He fears your influence and he is a realist. Perhaps our unfortunate conversation on the loggia reached the ears of the ill-disposed. We dare not waste a moment."

He turned to Phanocles.

"You will have to share our council. How fast can *Am-*

phitrite take us to Illyria?"

"Twice as fast as your triremes, Caesar."

"Mamillius, we are going together. I to convince him that I am still Emperor, you to convince him that you do not want to be one."

"But that will be dangerous!"

"Would you sooner stay and have your throat cut? I do not think Posthumus would allow you to commit suicide."

"And you?"

"Thank you, Mamillius. Amid all my worries I am touched. Let us start."

Phanocles pressed his fists to his forehead. The Emperor nodded to the quay and a procession of slaves began to cross the trireme with luggage. A little Syrian came hurrying from aft. He spoke quickly to Mamillius.

"Lord, it is impossible. There is nowhere for the Emperor to sleep. And look at the sky!"

There was no longer any blue to be seen. The sun was dispersed into a great patch of light that might soon be hidden completely.

"—and how am I to hold a course, lord, when I can no longer see the sky and there is no wind?"

"It is an order. Grandfather, let us get ashore for a moment at least."

"Why?"

"She is so dirty——"

"So are you, Mamillius. You stink."

The Syrian sidled up to the Emperor.

"If it is an order, Caesar, I will do my best. But first let us move the ship outside the harbour. You can transfer to her from your barge."

"It shall be so."

They crossed the trireme together. Mamillius ran to the tunnel with head averted from the women and disappeared. The Emperor went to where his barge was moored astern of the trireme and arranged himself comfortably under the baldachino. It was only then that he began to realize how ugly and preposterous the new ship was.

He shook his head gently.

"I am a very reluctant innovator."

The crowd of slaves aboard *Amphitrite* was being absorbed by her hold and the small crew was busily casting off. The crewmen of the trireme were bearing off with the looms of oars and she began to move sideways. Her cables splashed free in the water and were hauled aboard. The Emperor, under his shady purple, could see how the helmsman was heaving at the steering oars to bring her stern in and give her bows a sheer away from the trireme. Steam was jetting constantly from the brass belly over the furnace. Then he saw Phanocles stick his head out of the hold and wave the helmsman into stillness. He shouted something down to the bowels of the machine, the jet of steam increased till the scream of it rasped the air like a file then suddenly disappeared altogether. In answer a snarling roar rose from the ships and houses round the harbour till *Amphitrite* lay like some impossible lizard at bay in the centre of an arena.

The Emperor fanned himself with one hand.

"I have always considered a mob to be thoroughly predictable."

There came a grunt from the bowels of the ship and an iron clank. Talos moved all four hands, two back, two forward. Both wheels began to revolve slowly, port astern, starboard ahead. The blades of the paddles came down—smack, pause, smack!—so that dirty water shot from under them. They rose out of the water, throwing it high in the air, to fall back on the deck. The whole ship was streaming and steam rose in a cloud again, but this time from the hot surface of the sphere and the funnel. A great wailing came from her hold and Phanocles leapt on deck, to stand there, inspecting the deluge through screwed-up eyes as though he had never seen anything so interesting. *Amphitrite* was lying in one place, making no way, but turning; and the water sprayed up as from a fountain. Phanocles shouted down the hatch, the steam jetted up, the paddles creaked to a stop, and the water was running off her as though she had just come up from the bottom of the harbour. The noise from the people stormed at her as she lay in the centre of harbour with her steam jet screaming. There was a blink of light in the haze over the hills and almost immediately the thud of thunder.

The Emperor made a furtive sign with two fingers.

The lightning, however, was a divine irrelevance. As the Emperor shielded his eyes in expectation of *Amphitrite*'s destruction at the hands of an outraged Providence he glimpsed that she was not the only portent moving on the waters. Outside the harbour mouth but visible over the quay wall there was a solidity in the moving vapours. Before his mind had time to work he thought of it as the top of a rock or a low cliff. But the rock lengthened.

The Emperor scrambled ashore, crossed the quay and climbed the steps of the harbour wall where the women were sitting. The rock was clear of the mist. It was the prow and fo'castle of a great warship and from her hold came the measured beating of a drum. She was slightly off course for the entrance of the harbour but swinging already to bisect the narrow strip of water that lay between the two quays. Steadily she came on, sail furled on the yard, a crab suspended at either yard-arm, ejaculatory armament trained forrard, her decks glistening with steel and brass, the twenty-foot spear of her ram cutting the surface of the water like a shark. The drum tapped out a change of rhythm. The centipedal oars closed in aft as though they had been folded by a central intelligence. She slid through the entrance and her ram was in the harbour. The drums changed rhythm again. Pair after pair as they were free of the obstructing quays the oars unfolded, reversed, backed water. The Emperor saw a red and gold banner on the quarterdeck surmounted by a vindictive-looking eagle. He dropped down from the harbour wall, ignored the questions of the women and hurried back to his barge and the shelter of the baldachino.

Aboard *Amphitrite* they had noticed the warship too. The Emperor saw Phanocles and the captain gesticulating fiercely at each other. Phanocles ducked down the hatch, the jet of steam vanished and the paddles began to move. Immediately the captain ran along the deck, there was a flash of steel and *Amphitrite*'s anchor thumped into the water. But the drums were beating out another order. The oars of the warship rose and were rigid like spread wings. She glided forward with the last of her momentum like a vast and settling seabird. Her ram took *Amphitrite* under the starboard paddle and tore it. Men were swarming along the horizontal oars, leaping down, striking with sword hilts and the butts of spears. The growl of the harbour rose to a frantic cheer. Phanocles and the captain were hauled up between the oars and dumped on the warship's deck. Her oars began to move again so that the ram slid out of the torn wheel. *Amphitrite*, her wheels turning very slowly, began to revolve round her own anchor. The warship, starboard oars paddling ahead, port astern, was moving towards the quay where the trireme and the Emperor was.

The Emperor sat, pulling on his underlip. There were more moving cliffs outside the harbour, warships backing and filling, waiting to come in. There was another blink of light and clap of thunder but this time the Emperor did not notice it. Mamillius was standing on the quay by the barge in the attitude of one arrested at a moment of extreme haste. The Emperor, glancing sideways, was transfixed also.

Mamillius was dressed in armour. His breastplate flashed from a multitudinous and highly allegorical assembly of heroes and centaurs. A scarlet cloak dropped down his back to his heels. The red leather of his sword scabbard matched exactly the red leather openwork of the boots that reached nearly to his knees. The breastplate was matched in material and complexity by the brass helmet that he carried under his left arm.

The Emperor closed his eyes for a moment and spoke faintly.

"Bellona's bridegroom."

Mamillius seemed to collapse a little. He blushed.

"I thought—as we were going to the army—"

The Emperor surveyed the details of the uniform.

"I see that both Troy and Carthage have fallen."

The blush came and went, came again with a profuse perspiration.

"Do you know whose warship these are?"

"I——"

The Emperor rested his forehead on one hand.

"In the circumstances, a distaff would have been less open to misconstruction."

Always Mamillius kept the wall of his cloak between him and the women. He saw the gold and scarlet banner shake as the warship came alongside the trireme. Her ram lay alongside the barge. This time the colour left his face and did not return.

"What shall we do?"

"There is no time to do anything. Perhaps you might put your helmet on."

"It gives me a headache."

"Diplomacy," said the Emperor. "He has the soldiers—look at them! But we have the intelligence. It will be hard if we cannot smooth things over."

"What about me?"

"On the whole, I think you would be safer in China."

The emperor took Mamillius' hand and stepped ashore. He walked along the quay towards the warship with Mamillius at his heels. The crowd from her deck had flooded the trireme and was flowing across the quay so that the end by the harbour entrance was jammed full. There were prisoners, the abject and supplicating Syrian, slaves. Phanocles wearing an even wilder air of short-sighted bewilderment and soldiers, far too many soldiers. They bore huge bundles and bags that made them look as though they were about to contribute to a gigantic jumble sale. They were tricked out in favours of red and yellow. The loot of a countryside was suspended about them but they came to attention under their loads when they saw the purple fringe on the white toga. The Emperor stopped by the gangway and waited. Behind him the women were crouched by the harbour wall, veiled and terrified like a chorus of Trojan Women. Someone blew a large brass instrument on the warship, there was a clash of arms and the banner was dipped. A tall, dark figure, burly, armed and flashing, and full of intention, came striding down the gangway.

"Welcome home, Posthumus," said the Emperor, smiling. "You have saved us the trouble of coming to see you."

3

Jove's Own Bolt

Posthumus paused for a moment. His gold and scarlet plume waved a foot and a half above the Emperor's head. His olive-dark and broadly handsome face took on a look of calculation.

"Where have you hidden your troops?"

The Emperor raised his eyebrows.

"There are a few sentries in the garden as usual and possibly a few by the tunnel. Really, Posthumus, you travel with a considerable retinue."

Posthumus turned aside and spoke briefly among his officers. A detachment of laden legionaries doubled along the quay and stationed themselves between the Emperor and escape. The women wailed then settled to a steady lament. The Emperor affected not to notice but drew Posthumus towards the barge. *Amphitrite* continued to circle round her anchor slowly.

Posthumus stopped.

"It was high time I came home."

More thunder. The Emperor looked back at the dense mass of soldiers that filled the end of the quay.

"About a hundred men, I should say. An Imperial Salute?"

Posthumus snorted.

"You can call it that. Presently more ships will enter the harbour. There will be sufficient to ensure that we agree on all points of policy. But what a stroke of luck to find you both on the quay!"

Mamillius cleared his throat and spoke in a high uncertain voice.

"Posthumus, you are mistaken."

"Mamillius in arms."

"For show only. I do not want to be Emperor."

"Ah!"

Posthumus took a step towards him and Mamillius started back, tripping on his cloak. Posthumus poked a finger in his face.

"You may think not. But he would bridge the Adriatic to please you."

The Emperor flushed a delicate pink.

"You have never wanted my affection, Posthumus, so you have never missed it. If I have been foolish enough to think that I could enjoy his company without more danger than the usual scandal, I have been wise enough to know that you are the best man to rule the Empire—however uncongenial I may find you."

"I am informed otherwise."

"At least you might gloss over our differences in public."

Posthumus paid no attention to these words, but fished a folded paper from inside his breastplate.

"To:

Posthumus, etc., Heir Designate, etc.

From:

CIII

Ships and weapons are being built or converted on the quay next to the tunnel. The Emperor and the Lord Mamillius take much personal interest in a ship, *Amphitrite*, ex-corn-barge, unclassified, and a tormentum (mark VII) that has been placed on the quay and trained seaward. They are also experimenting with methods of poisoning food on a large scale. Lord Mamillius seems to be in a state of high excitement and anticipation——"

"Posthumus, I swear——"

Posthumus merely raised his voice.

"He is corresponding with the Emperor and others in code under cover of writing poetry——"

Mamillius was flaming.

"Leave my poetry alone!"

"It has not yet been found possible to break this code. Submitted to XLVI; it proved to be composed of quotations from Moschus, Erinna, Mimnermus, and sources not yet identified. Research is proceeding."

Tears of rage ran down Mamillius' face.

"You filthy swine!"

"That was unnecessarily cruel, Posthumus."

Posthumus stuffed the paper back.

"Now we have done with fooling, Caesar. The time has come for a regency."

"He does not want to be Emperor."

Posthumus sneered at Mamillius.

"He is not going to be."

A faint clattering sound came from Mamillius' armour. The Emperor laid a hand on Posthumus' arm.

"If the ship and the tormentum worry you, Posthumus, I can explain them rationally. Be fair."

He turned to the officers and raised his voice.

"Bring the Greek to me."

Posthumus nodded, waiting. Phanocles stood before them, restoring the circulation to his wrists.

"This man is the root of the matter."

"Lord Posthumus—I am altering the shape of the world."

"He has this curious manner of speech, Posthumus."

"There will be no slaves but coal and iron. The ends of the earth will be joined together."

Posthumus laughed and the sound cheered no one.

"And men will fly."

He turned to the officers and beckoned.

"Colonel—why aren't those ships coming in?"

"Visibility, sir."

"Damn the visibility. Signal them in or send a message."

He turned back to Phanocles.

"This fantastic ship——"

Phanocles spread his arms.

"She will go faster than any other. Civilization is a matter of communications." He frowned at them and searched for simple words. "Lord Posthumus. You are a soldier. What is your greatest difficulty?"

"I have none."

"But if you had?"

"Getting there first."

"You see? Even warfare is a matter of communications. Think of the elaborate efforts Xerxes made to conquer Greece. With *Amphitrite* he could have crossed the Aegean in a day and against the wind."

Mamillius struck in, teeth chattering, eager to help.

"Think of the first Caesar, of Alexander, Rameses——"

Phanocles sank his head on one side and opened his hands as if the explanation was simple.

"You see, lord? Communications."

The Emperor nodded thoughtfully.

"They should be made as difficult as possible."

Thunder rumbled again. Posthumus strode over to the tormentum and the women shrank away. The roar of the harbour was rising again.

"And this?"

"I have to shut the lightning in the keg. The sting when it strikes anything looses the lightning. Then there is a smoking hole in the ground."

The Emperor made a sign with two fingers.

"What is the brass butterfly at the base of the sting?"

"It is an arming vane. After the keg has gone some way the butterfly shoots off, otherwise the keg would explode by setback when you fired the tormentum."

"Would this make a smoking hole where there was a city wall?"

"Yes, Caesar."

"Where there was an army?"

"If I make the keg big enough."

Posthumus considered Phanocles closely.

"And this is the only one you have made?"

"Yes, lord."

"I am not sure whether to have you executed straight away or use you for other purposes."

"——Execute me?"

Suddenly the roar from the harbour rose till it could no longer be ignored.

They turned together.

It was *Amphitrite*; they understood that immediately. She had revolved endlessly round her anchor till her flaunted eccentricity had become more than any man could bear who had red blood in his veins. There were naked men plunging from ships and jetties till a hundred arms flashed in the water.

Phanocles cried out.

"What——?"

Posthumus spoke rapidly to the Colonel.

"All troops will disembark on this quay. Meanwhile neither the Emperor nor his suite will wish to leave. See that his wishes are respected. You understand?"

"Sir."

Posthumus ran to the barge but the Emperor called to him.

"While I am waiting I will inspect these splendid fellows already assembled."

The colonel glanced at Posthumus, who laughed softly.

"Do as the Father Of His Country tells you."

The arc of swimmers converged on *Amphitrite* and the second warship was coming in to the sound of drums. Phanocles clasped his hands.

"Stop them, Caesar!"

Men were swarming now over *Amphitrite*, tearing at her paddle, striking with any heavy gear they could find at the brass monster in the deck. The guard that Posthumus had put aboard her went down in a whirl of limbs. Smoke rose suddenly from her hold and uncoiled. Naked figures were hurling themselves from her bulwarks while a thin flame, hooded and flickering like a ghost, shot up amidships. The second warship saw the danger and backed water. Oars smashed against the quay but her way was checked. A third ship, emerging from the heat haze crashed into the second with her ram. More oars smashed; then both ships were locked and drifting helplessly down on *Amphitrite*. Posthumus, screaming curses, leapt into the imperial barge.

"Bear off there! Give way!"

"Detachment ready for inspection, Caesar."

"Those men between me and the tunnel, Colonel. Let them join the others."

"My orders, Caesar——"

"Do you not think, Colonel, that you could catch half a dozen women and one old man if they tried to escape?"

The Colonel swallowed.

"This may be the last time the Father Of His Country will inspect his troops. Will you not obey, Colonel? I am a soldier too."

The Colonel's Adam's apple went up and down twice. He swelled with understanding and emotion. He flashed the Emperor an enormous salute.

"Detail to join parade at the double!"

"And the band," added the Emperor. "I think I see the band there. The band, Colonel?"

A fourth warship was gliding into the harbour. *Amphitrite* lay, her brass boiler nested in smoke and flame. Her paddle wheels began to lumber round faster. She strained at her cable. They heard a wild scream from Posthumus.

"Back water, curse you!"

Flutes, buccinas, tubas. The brass tube of each *lituus* was wound round the waist and projected in an elephantine bell over the shoulder. Drums, kettle and bass. Scarlet and gold.

The parade filled the end of the jetty and faced the trireme. The band formed up between the parade and the tormentum. The women wrung their hands. *Amphitrite* was revolving and flailing up flames and smoke. The fourth warship was trying to circle round her and the other two. But a fifth was about to enter the harbour.

"Band!"

Amphitrite was moving faster. A fathom or two of her cable eased out and she fetched a wider circle, brushed the locked warships so that their rigging flamed. Posthumus was jumping up and down.

"Use your crabs!"

Amphitrite veered another fathom or two of cable. Her circle included the imperial barge which got under way with extraordinary lack of ceremony. Round she went, round and round, with Posthumus screaming and *Amphitrite* breathing fire down her neck.

The band struck up.

"Open order, Colonel?"

The Colonel quivered.

"There is no room, Caesar. They would step straight down between the quay and the trireme."

"In that case," said the Emperor, "they will have to carry their impedimenta and loot or I shall not be able to walk between the ranks."

The band began to countermarch between the main detachment and the tormentum, ten paces forward, ten paces back. They were splendid. The men were splendid. The seamen were splendid aboard their utterly splendid ships. The women felt the men were splendid and that if

211

they themselves were in danger from General Posthumus it was worth it. Chests swelled, bosoms heaved, and calves quivered. Mamillius put his helmet on.

The Emperor paused by the left-hand man of the first rank.

"And how long have you been in the army, my man?"

Amphitrite's cable charred through and snapped. Her turning circle became a wide sweep. She touched one of the trots of merchantmen moored by the warehouses and immediately they were dressed overall with flame.

"Somebody use a crab!"

All at once every man in every ship was possessed by one idea—to get out of the harbour. A burning warship limped astern past the end of the quay and the heat from her scorched the parade. Outside *Amphitrite's* dreadful arc the water was hidden by ships great and small that fought each other and strove for the safety of the haze-covered sea. Over all this the thunder rolled, dropping bright light into the hills and the band played.

"Where did you get that scar? A jab with a spear? A bottle, eh?"

The legionaires stood rigidly to attention under their sixty-four pounds of brass, their impedimenta, their loot, and the dreadful heat. The Colonel watched a drop of sweat forming on the tip of his nose till his eyes crossed. The Emperor spoke to each man in the front rank.

There was a mess of warships revolving in the centre of the harbour with *Amphitrite* nuzzling them. The captain of one of them was facing Posthumus at the salute. At that moment either a cable charred through or someone, in blind obedience, used a crab. A black star-shaped hole appeared on the quarter-deck where the captain had been. He went down with his ship.

"How tall are you? Do you like the army? Where did you get that dint from? A slingstone? I should have said a slingstone, shouldn't you, Colonel? Don't ever let the Quartermaster issue you with a new shield, my man. Tell him the Emperor said so. How many children have you got? None? We must arrange some leave after this inspection."

The word "leave" spread. The legionaries stiffened to endure but already some of them were swaying. The Emperor moved along the front rank with awful deliberation.

"Don't I remember you from the IXth? In Greece? Why haven't you been promoted? Look into that, Colonel, will you?"

A second warship was extracting herself from the harbour among a mass of smaller shipping. *Amphitrite* was bearing down on the harbour mouth in pursuit of the Emperor's barge.

"What are you going to have done for that boil, my man? Here's what I call a really impressive fellow. How on earth he can support those three bundles I don't know. What's your name?"

Suddenly there was a gap of air in front of the Emperor and a brazen crash. The legionary had passed out.

"As I was saying, we must arrange some leave for them now that the Heir has brought them home to their Father."

"Caesar——"

"Where did you lose that eye, my man? Don't lose the other, will you?"

Crash.

Oil was spilling from a warehouse and burning on the water. A thick cloud of black smoke drifted across the parade.

The Emperor spoke softly to the Colonel.

"You see how comedy and tragedy are mingled. Whose orders will you take? These men ought to be putting out the fires."

The Colonel's eyes uncrossed for a moment.

"I have my orders, Caesar."

"Very well. Now, my man, how do you like the army? Has it made a man of you?"

Crash.

"Discipline," said the Emperor to the right-hand man, "is a great convenience."

"Caesar?"

"I should have said a splendid thing of course."

He stood looking down into the sooty water of the harbour entrance. A constant flow of singed traffic was passing before him. The band drowned the language that came from it, but judging from the contorted faces it was complex and personal. *Amphitrite* and the imperial barge came through almost together.

"Tell me, sergeant, if I gave the orders 'Right turn, quick march' would you obey me?"

But the sergeant was an old soldier, mahogany-coloured and indestructible. His loot was worth all the rest on the quay, but it was in a tiny bag suspended under his breastplate. Even so the sweat ran off him.

"In the 'oggin, armour an' all, Caesar?" For a moment the disciplined eyes flickered sideways and down. "I'd be glad to."

It was not only the smoke and sweat that threw up a meditative gleam in the Emperor's eye.

"Sir! Caesar!"

The words burst from the Colonel. His sword was vibrating and the veins in his neck were swelling like ivy-branches. The Emperor smiled peacefully and turned to worm his way between the ranks. It was like being in a tunnel under the huge bundles, in the thick air and before the row of bulging eyes. But there were a number of airholes already where Posthumus' chosen men lay flat on their backs, keeled over on parade. The little trail of men, the Colonel, Mamillius, Phanocles, wormed after the Emperor. The panic uproar of the town, the harbour and the shipping was punctuated by the brazen fall of legionaries.

Outside the harbour the warships were disappearing into the heat haze and all the small ships were trying to get back in. *Amphitrite* was moving more slowly. As the heat built up round her boiler she would make a clumsy advance between her flailing paddles. But the paddles threw up so much water that this movement dampened down the fire again and she would slow to a stop. So she wove a complex and unpredictable pattern over the water in a series of clownish lunges. She was settling low in the water.

The band continued to play.

Crash. Crash. Crash.

March and counter-march, worm between the thinning ranks. The Watch on the Rhine, Entry of the Gladiators, Guardians of the Wall, the Old Cth, excerpts from The Burning of Rome and The Boys We Left Behind Us. The tenements were on fire, their washing flaming like the rigging of ships. In the warehouses wine burnt brightly but corn only smouldered and stank.

"And now," said the Emperor, "I will address them." He climbed the harbour wall and stood for a moment fanning himself. "Will you turn them about, Colonel?"

The band fell in, the town burned, *Amphitrite* sank, hissing. The townspeople were outward bound for the open country. It was a scene of godlike and impersonal destruction.

Crash.

"—have watched you with growing pride. You evince in these decadent modern times the spirit that made Rome great. Yours not to reason why, yours but to obey your master's voice."

Mamillius, standing at the foot of the wall, could see the shadows of the Emperor and the Colonel on the quay at his feet. One of them was swaying gently backwards and forwards.

"Under the weight of the sun, the joyous oppression of sixty-four pounds of brass, bearing on your shoulders the heavy fruits of your labours you have stood and endured because you were ordered to. This is what we expect of our soldiers."

Mamillius began to work his feet heel and toe as he had learned to do as a child. He looked straight before him but moved smoothly and unnoticeably away from the inspection. Soon the women and the sheltering bulk of the tormentum hid him.

"Ships burned before your eyes. A town was laid waste by pitiless fire. Reason told you to put the flames out. The common and undisciplined dictates of humanity whispered to you that women and children, the aged and the sick required your assistance. But you are soldiers and you had your orders. I congratulate Rome on her children."

Mamillius had vanished. The women were disposed in a graceful group between the parade and the tunnel. The Colonel found he could see nothing but two swords that drifted farther and farther apart. He put his left hand cautiously under his right wrist to steady them.

The Emperor reminded the troops of Roman history.

Romulus and Remus.

Crash.

Manlius, Horatius. The Standard Bearer of the IXth.

Crash.

The Emperor traced the expansion of the Empire, the manly virtues which they so admirably exemplified. He outlined the history of Greece, its decadence; touched on Egyptian sloth.

Crash. Crash.

Suddenly the Colonel was no longer at his side on the seawall. There came one loud plop from the sea and no more. The Colonel's armour was heavy.

The Emperor talked about battle honours.

Crash.

Out of the mist, perhaps half a mile from the harbour, the imperial barge appeared again. Her oars beat very, very slowly as she made for the entrance.

The crest of the legion.

Crash.

The honour of the legion.

The point of crisis, of no return, had been reached. The movement began at the Emperor's feet where three men fell together. A wave of sick nausea swept over the parade and the ranks went down together into merciful unconsciousness. The end of the quay was piled with a hundred helpless men and a band that could hear nothing over the beating of its own devoted hearts. The Emperor looked down at them compassionately.

"Self-preservation."

Mamillius and the Emperor's guard broke from the tunnel. There were perhaps two dozen of them, men fresh from a kip in the shady garden and agreeable now to a little brisk brutality. Mamillius was flourishing his sword, chanting a bloodcurdling chorus from the *Seven Against Thebes* and trying to keep step to it. At the same moment the imperial barge thumped the quay. Posthumus, dirty, dishevelled and raging, scrambled ashore. The Emperor's guard broke formation, ran forward and seized him. He threw two off and leapt at Mamillius with drawn sword, roaring like a bull. Mamillius stopped in his tracks, hands and knees pressed together, chin up. He abandoned Greek for his native tongue.

"Pax——!"

Posthumus swung his sword and the Emperor closed his eyes. He heard a gong-like sound and opened them again. Posthumus was heaving under a mob of guards. Mamillius was staggering in a circle, trying unsuccessfully to push his helmet up off his eyes.

"You rotten cad, Posthumus, you absolute outsider! Now I shall have a headache."

The Emperor got down from the sea wall.

"Who is the man Posthumus brought with him in the barge?"

The Officer of the Guard saluted.

"A prisoner, Caesar. A slave, by the looks of him."

The Emperor tapped the finger of one hand in the palm of the other.

"Escort the Heir Designate through the tunnel, and the slave with him. Two of your men can lead the

Lord Mamillius. This is not the moment to extract him. Ladies, the demonstration is over. You may return to the Villa."

He paused for a moment by the tormentum and looked back at the quay. The guard of honour and the band were stirring feebly like sea-creatures of the shore at the return of the tide.

"Six of your men must hold the tunnel at all costs. They must not stand aside except at your personal order."

"Caesar."

"The remainder can stand by in the garden. Keep them out of sight behind the hedges, at the double."

"Caesar."

The gardens had retained their tranquillity. The Emperor stood by the lily-pond, breathing the aromatic air grate-fully. Below him the surface of the sea had begun to appear again. When his breathing was even he turned to the little group of men.

"Will you behave, Posthumus, if I tell the guard to let you go?"

Posthumus glanced at the dark mouth of the tunnel and the Emperor shook his head.

"Please put the idea of bolting through the tunnel out of your head. The men there have their orders. Come! Let us discuss things reasonably."

Posthumus shook himself free.

"What have you done to my soldiers you—sorcerer?"

"Just an inspection, Posthumus, just the usual line. But I produced it to infinity."

Posthumus reached up and settled his helmet. The scarlet and gold plume was singed.

"What are you going to do with me?"

The Emperor smiled wryly.

"Look at Mamillius. Can you imagine him as an Emperor?"

Mamillius was lying across a stone seat on his stomach. Two soldiers held his legs. At the other end a third soldier was heaving back on the jammed helmet.

"The agent's reports were circumstantial."

The Emperor crooked his finger.

"Phanocles."

"Caesar."

"Tell the Heir Designate once and for all what you were going to do."

"I told him, Caesar. No slaves, no war."

Posthumus sneered.

"Bring the slave I caught. He was one of those who burned your ship."

Two soldiers frog-marched the slave forward. He was naked, though the water had dried off him. He was a man to tear a lion apart, bearded, broad, dark and wild.

The Emperor looked him up and down.

"What is he?"

A soldier seized the man's hair, twisted his head sideways

221

and up so that he grinned with pain. Posthumus leaned forward and inspected the notches cut in the slave's ear. He nodded and the soldier let go.

"Why did you do it?"

The slave answered him in a voice at once hoarse with shouting and clumsy with disuse.

"I am a rower."

The Emperor's eyebrows climbed.

"In future I must have rowers chained to their oars, or would that be too expensive?"

The slave tried to clasp his hands.

"Caesar—be merciful. We could not kill that man."

"Phanocles?"

"His demon protected him. A plank killed the slave by his side. The crab missed him."

Mamillius came out of his helmet with a shriek. He hurried to the Emperor.

"Mamillius—the crab was not meant for you!"

Mamillius turned excitedly to the slave.

"You did not try to kill me?"

"Why should we, lord? If you use us up, you have a right to. We were bought. But this man does not use us at all. We saw his ship move without oars or sails and against the wind. What use will there be for rowers?"

Phanocles cried out.

"My ship would have set you free!"

The Emperor looked down at the slave thoughtfully.

"Are you happy on your bench?"

222

"The gods know what we suffer."

"Why then?"

The slave paused for a moment. When he spoke again the words came by rote out of some deep well of the past.

"'I had rather be slave to a smallholder than rule in hell over all the ghosts of men.'"

"I see."

The Emperor nodded to the soldiers.

"Take him away."

Posthumus laughed unpleasantly.

"That was what a professional sailor thinks of your ship, Greek!"

The Emperor raised his voice.

"Wait. Let us have the verdict of a professional soldier on the thunder-machine. Officer!"

But the officer was already saluting.

"Excuse me, Caesar, but the lady——"

"What lady?"

"They won't let her pass without my orders, Caesar."

Mamillius shouted in his broken voice.

"Euphrosyne!"

The officer came down from the salute.

"Let the lady pass, lads. Jump to it!"

The soldiers parted from the end of the tunnel and Euphrosyne came, hurrying and shrinking, to Phanocles and the Emperor.

"Where have you been, child? Why weren't you with the others? The quay is dangerous without me!"

But she still said nothing, and the veil shook against her mouth. The Emperor beckoned.

"Stand by me. You are safe now."

He turned back to the officer.

"Officer."

"Caesar."

"Stand easy. Posthumus, ask your questions."

Posthumus surveyed him for a moment.

"Captain. Do you enjoy the prospect of a battle?"

"In defence of the Father of his Country——"

The Emperor waved his hand.

"Your loyalty is not in question. Answer, please."

The Captain thought.

"On the whole, yes, Caesar."

"Why?"

"Makes a change, Caesar. Excitement, promotion, perhaps loot—and so on."

"Would you prefer to destroy your enemies at a distance?"

"I don't understand."

Posthumus jerked a thumb sideways at Phanocles.

"This slimy Greek has made that weapon on the quay. You press the tit and the enemy goes up in smoke."

The Captain ruminated.

"Has the Father of his Country no further use for his soldiers, then?"

Posthumus looked meaningly at the Captain.

"Apparently not. But I have."

"But sir—suppose the enemy gets this thunder-machine himself?"

Posthumus looked at Phanocles.

"Will armour be any use?"

"None, I should say."

The Emperor took Mamillius by the scarlet cloak and tugged it gently.

"I imagine this sort of uniform will disappear. You will spend your war crawling round on your belly. Your uniform will be mud- or dung-coloured."

The officer glanced down at his glittering breastplate.

"—and you could always paint the metal a neutral tint or just let it get dirty."

The officer paled.

"You are joking, Caesar."

"You saw what his ship did in the harbour."

The officer stepped back. His mouth was open and he was breathing quickly like a man in the first stages of nightmare. He began to glance round him, at the hedges, the stone seats, the soldiers blocking the tunnel——

Posthumus strode forward and grasped him by the arm.

"Well, Captain?"

Their eyes met. Doubt left the Captain's face. His jaw jutted and the muscles of his cheeks stood out.

"Can you manage the others, General?"

Posthumus nodded.

Instantly there was a confusion. Through a frieze of gesticulating figures, through an entanglement of men who sought to save their balance on the edge of the pond, Phanocles was visible sailing away from Posthumus' fist out over the quiet lilies. Then the officer was running fast toward the entrance of the tunnel and Posthumus was lumbering behind him. The officer shouted an order at the men guarding the entrance and they sidestepped like a human screen—one, two! one, two! one, two! Posthumus and the officer vanished into the tunnel and the guard remained to one side at attention. The soldiers began to sort themselves out by the pool. Mamillius, who had the whole width of the pool between him and the tunnel, was dashing this way and that as his astonished mind tried to find the quickest way round it. Only the Emperor still silent and distinguished, a little paler, perhaps, a little more remote as the certainty of downfall and death settled on him. Then the soldiers had picked themselves up, Phanocles had clambered out of the pool through which Mamillius, his problem solved, was now wading. Hesitating and unbelieving at the officer's defection they converged on the mouth of the tunnel. The Emperor strolled after them. He gazed thoughtfully at the human screen that discipline had rendered so ineffective. He shrugged slightly inside his toga.

He spoke very gently, as to children.

"You may stand easy."

A sudden push of air through the tunnel moved them and let them go. Almost at the same moment the ground jumped and noise hit them like the blow of a fist. The Emperor turned to Mamillius.

"Thunder?"

"Vesuvius?"

There was a whining sound from the air over the headland that separated the garden from the port, a descending whine, a brazen clang near at hand and the whisper of yew branches. The timeless moment of shock dulled for them the immediacy of their danger so that they looked at each other foolishly. Phanocles was shaking. Then there were footsteps in the tunnel, coming hastily, running, staggering. A soldier burst out of the entrance and they saw from the red and yellow favour that he was one of Posthumus' men.

"Caesar——"

"Pull yourself together. Then make your report."

"He is dead——"

"Who is dead and how did it happen?"

The soldier swayed back, then recovered.

"How can I tell you, Caesar? We were getting fell in again after the—after the inspection. General Posthumus came running from the tunnel. He saw that some of our company were away fighting the fires and he began to call out to the rest of us. There was one of your officers running behind him. I saw the officer bend down by the mark VII. There was a flash of lightning, a thunder-clap——"

"And a smoking hole in the quay. Where is Posthumus?"

The soldier spread his arms in a gesture of ignorance.

227

Phanocles fell on his knees and put out a hand to the hem of the Emperor's toga. But the soldier was looking past them to the nearer yew hedge between the pool and the ascent of the gardens. They saw his eyes widen terribly. He screamed and took to his heels.

"Sorcery!"

Posthumus was watching them, must be watching them from behind the yew hedge, for they could see his bronze helmet with the scarlet and gold plume on it. He appeared to be cooking a small meal, for the air above his helmet shook with more than summer's heat. They saw that the plume was turning slowly to brown. The sprigs of yew bent, curled in the heat, gave way. The helmet bowed, turned among the branches and hung with its empty interior towards them.

"Come here, my man."

The soldier crept out of hiding.

"The All-Father has destroyed General Posthumus before the eyes of you and your companions for the sin of open rebellion against the Emperor. Tell them."

He turned to Phanocles.

"Go and save what you can. You are heavily in debt with humanity. Go with them, Mamillius, for you are in charge. There is an occasion waiting for you through the tunnel. Rise to it."

Their steps echoed in the tunnel and died away.

"Come, lady."

He sat down on one of the stone seats by the lily-pool.

"Stand before me."

She came, stood, but the grace of movement was gone.

"Give it me."

For a while she said nothing, but stood defended by her draperies. The Emperor said nothing but allowed the silent authority of his outstretched hand to do its work. Then she shoved the thing at him, left it in his hand and raised her own to her hidden face. The Emperor looked down at his palm thoughtfully.

"I owe my life to you it seems. Not that Posthumus wouldn't have made a better job of ruling. Lady, I must see your face."

She said nothing, did nothing. The Emperor watched her, then nodded as though they had been in explicit communion.

"I understand."

He got up, walked round the pool and stood looking over the cliff at the now visible waves.

"Let this remain another bit of history that is better forgotten."

He pitched the brass butterfly into the sea.

4

L'Envoy

The Emperor and Phanocles lay opposite each other on either side of a low table. The table, the floor, the room, were circular and surrounded by pillars that held up a shadowy cupola. A constellation hung glittering in the opening directly over their heads but the room itself was lit softly from lights placed behind the pillars—warm light, congenial to leisure and digestion. A flute meditated somewhere.

"Will it work, do you think?"

"Why not, Caesar?"

"Strange man. You ponder thus and thus on universal law and evolve a certainty. Of course it will work. I must be patient."

They were silent for a while. The eunuch voice joined and commented on the flute.

"What was Mamillius doing when you left him, Phanocles?"

"He was giving many orders."

"Excellent."

"They were the wrong orders, but men were obeying him."

"That is the secret. He will be a terrible Emperor. Better than Caligula but less talented than Nero."

"He was so proud of the scar in his helmet. He said he had discovered that he was a man of action."

"So much for poetry. Poor Mamillius."

"No, Caesar. He said that action brought out the poet in him and that he had created the perfect poem in action."

"Not an epic, surely?"

"An epigram, Caesar. 'Euphrosyne is beautiful but dumb.'"

The Emperor inclined his head gravely.

"Whereas you and I know that she is extremely clever and quick-witted."

Phanocles lifted a little on his couch.

"How could you know that?"

The Emperor rolled a grape backwards and forwards under his finger.

"I shall marry her, of course. Do not gape at me, Phanocles, or fear that I shall have you strangled when I see her face. At my age, unfortunately, it will be a marriage in name only. But it will give her security and secrecy and a measure of peace. She has a harelip, has she not?"

The blood suffused Phanocles' face, seemed to drown him and make his eyes bolt. The Emperor wagged a finger.

"Only a young fool like Mamillius could mistake her pathological shyness for a becoming modesty. I whisper this down to you from the pinnacle of a long experience and hope no woman may hear: but we men invented modesty. I wonder if we invented chastity as well? No beautiful woman could possibly refuse to show her face for so long if it were unblemished."

"I did not dare tell you."

"Because you saw that I entertained you for her sake? Alas for Mamillius and romantic love. Perseus and Andromeda! How he will dislike me. I ought to have remembered from the first that an Emperor cannot enjoy a normal human relationship."

"I am sorry——"

"So am I, Phanocles, and not wholly for myself. Did you never think to turn the light of your extraordinary intellect on Medicine?"

"No, Caesar."

"Shall I tell you why?"

"I am listening."

The Emperor's words were clear and gentle, dropping in the quiet room like tiny stones.

"I said you are hubristic. You are also selfish. You are alone in your universe with natural law and people are an interruption, an intrusion. I am selfish too and alone—but with the shape of people acknowledged to have a certain right to independent existence. Oh, you natural philosophers! Are there many of you, I wonder? Your single-minded and devoted selfishness, your royal preoccupation with the only thing that can interest you, could go near to wiping life off the earth as I wipe the bloom from this grape."

His nostrils quivered.

"But silence now. Here comes the trout."

However, there was a ritual of this too, entry of the major-domo and the service, more patterns of movement. The Emperor broke his own commandment.

"Are you too young, I wonder? Or do you find as I do, that when you read a book you once liked, half the pleasure is evocation of the time when you first read it? You see how selfish I am, Phanocles! If I were to read the eclogues I should not be transported to a Roman Arcady. I should be a boy again, preparing the next day's passage for my tutor."

Phanocles was recovering.

"A poor return for reading, Caesar."

"Do you think so? Surely we selfish men comprise all history in our own lives! Each of us discovers the pyramids. Space, time, life—what I might call the four-dimensional continuum—but you see how ill-adapted Latin is to philosophy! Life is a personal matter with a single fixed point of reference. Alexander did not fight his wars until I discovered him at the age of seven. When I was a baby, time was an instant; but I pushed, smelled, tasted, saw, heard, bawled that one suffocating point into whole palaces of history and vast fields of space."

"Again I do not understand you, Caesar."

"You should, for I report on an experience common to us both. But you lack my introversion—or shall I say selfishness?—see how prone an uninterrupted Emperor is to parenthesis!—and therefore you cannot distinguish it. Think, Phanocles! If you can restore to me not the gratification of an appetite, but a single precious memory! How else but by the enlargements of anticipation and memory does our human instant differ from the mindless movement of nature's clock?"

Phanocles glanced up at the constellation that hung so near and bright that they might have thought it deepened by a third dimension; but before he could think of anything to say the dishes were in place. The covers were lifted, and the sweet steam came with them. The Emperor closed his eyes, held his head forward and breathed in.

"Yes——?"

Then in accents of profound emotion:

"Yes!"

Phanocles ate his trout quickly, for he was hungry, and wished that the Emperor would give him a chance to drink too. But the Emperor was in a trance. His lips were moving and the colour came and went in his face.

"Freshness. Levels of shining water and shadows and cataracts from the dark rock on high.

"It comes back to me. I am lying on a rock that is only just as big as my body. The cliffs rise about me, the river runs by me and the water is dark for all the sun. Two

234

pigeons discourse musically and monotonously. There is pain in my right side, for the edge of the rock cuts me: but I lie face-downward, my right arm moving slowly as a water-snail on a lump of stone. I touch a miracle of present actuality, I stroke—I am fiercely, passionately alive—a moment more and the exultation of my heart will burst in a fury of movement. But I still my ambition, my desire, my lust—I balance passion with will. I stroke slowly as a drifting weed. She lies there in the darkness, undulating, stemming the flow of water. Now—! A convulsion of two bodies, sense of terror, of rape—she flies in the air and I grab with lion's claws. She is out, she is mine———"

The Emperor opened his eyes and looked across at Phanocles. A tear trickled on his cheek exactly above the untasted fish.

"—my first trout."

He seized a cup, spilt a drop or two on the floor then held the cup up towards Phanocles.

"To the pressure cooker. The most Promethean discovery of them all."

After a while he mastered his emotion and laughed a little.

"I wonder how I am to reward you?"

"Caesar!"

Phanocles gulped and spluttered.

"My explosive———"

"I take no account of the steamship. She is amusing

235

but expensive. I must admit that the experimentalist in me was interested in her atrocious activities, but once is enough. You must make no more steamships."

"But Caesar!"

"Besides, how can you find your way without a wind?"

"I might invent a mechanism which pointed constantly in one direction."

"By all means invent it. Perhaps you could invent a movable arrow that pointed constantly to Rome."

"Something that would point to the North."

"But no more steamships."

"I——"

The Emperor waved his hand.

"It is our Imperial will, Phanocles."

"I bow."

"She was dangerous."

"Perhaps one day, Caesar, when men are free because they no longer believe themselves to be slaves——"

The Emperor shook his head.

"You work among perfect elements and therefore politically you are an idealist. There will always be slaves though the name may change. What is slavery but the domination of the weak by the strong? How can you make them equal? Or are you fool enough to think that men are born equal?"

He was suddenly grave.

"As for your explosive—it has preserved me this day and therefore the peace of the Empire. But it has cost the

Empire a merciless ruler who would have murdered half a dozen people and given justice to a hundred million. The world has lost a bargain. No, Phanocles. We will restore Jove's own bolt to his random and ineluctable hand."

"But they were my greatest inventions!"

The first trout had disappeared, cold from the Emperor's plate. Another had descended and again he immersed his face in its fragrance.

"The pressure cooker. I shall reward you for that."

"Then, Caesar, how will you reward me for this?"

"For what?"

"My third invention. I have kept it in reserve."

His hand went slowly, dramatically, to his belt. The Emperor watched him apprehensively.

"Has this any connection with thunder?"

"With silence only."

The Emperor frowned. He held a paper in either hand and glanced from one to the other.

"Poems? You are a poet then?"

"Mamillius wrote it."

"I might have known. Sophocles, Carcides—how well read the boy is!"

"This will make him famous. Read the other poem, Caesar, for it is exactly the same. I have invented a method of multiplying books. I call it printing."

"But this is—another pressure cooker!"

"A man and a boy can make a thousand copies of a book in a day."

The Emperor looked up from the two papers.

"We could give away a hundred thousand copies of Homer!"

"A million if you like."

"No poet need pine for lack of an audience——"

"Nor for money. No more dictating an edition to a handful of slaves. Caesar. A poet will sell his poems by the sack like vegetables. The very scullions will solace themselves with the glories of our Athenian drama——"

The Emperor rose to a sitting position in his enthusiasm.

"A Public Library in every town!"

"——in every home."

"Ten thousand copies of the love poems of Catullus——"

"A hundred thousand of the works of Mamillius——"

"Hesiod in every cottage——"

"An author in every street——"

"An alpine range of meticulous inquiry and information on every conceivable topic——"

"Knowledge, education——"

The Emperor lowered himself again.

"Wait. Is there enough genius to go round? How often is a Horace born?"

"Come, Caesar. Nature is bountiful."

"Supposing we all write books?"

"Why not? Interesting biographies——"

The Emperor was gazing intently at a point out of this

world—somewhere in the future.

"Diary of a Provincial Governor. I Built Hadrian's Wall. My Life in Society, by a Lady of Quality."

"Scholarship, then."

"Fifty interpolated passages in the catalogue of ships. Metrical innovations in the Mimes of Herondas. The Unconscious Symbolism of the first book of Euclid. Prologomena to the Investigation of Residual Trivia."

Terror appeared in the Emperor's eyes.

"History—In the Steps of Thucydides. I was Nero's Grandmother."

Phanocles sat up and clapped his hands enthusiastically.

"Reports, Caesar, essential facts!"

The terror grew.

"—Military, Naval, Sanitary, Eugenic—I shall have to read them all! Political, Economic, Pastoral, Horticultural, Personal, Impersonal, Statistical, Medical——"

The Emperor staggered to his feet. His hands were lifted, his eyes were shut and his face was contorted.

"Let him sing again!"

Masterful and unimpassioned.

The Emperor opened his eyes. He went quickly to one of the pillars and stroked the factual stone for reassurance. He looked up to the ceiling and gazed at the tiled constellation that hung, sparkling, in the crystal spheres. He calmed himself though his body still shivered slightly. He turned and looked across at Phanocles.

"But we were speaking of your reward."

239

"I am in Caesar's hands."

The Emperor came close and looked at him with quivering lips.

"Would you like to be an ambassador?"

"My highest ambition has never——"

"You would have time then to invent your instrument which points to the North. You can take your explosive and your printing with you. I shall make you Envoy Extraordinary and Plenipotentiary."

He paused for a moment.

"Phanocles, my dear friend. I want you to go to China."

The novels of William Golding

ff

Lord of the Flies

A plane crashes on a desert island and the only survivors, a group of schoolboys, assemble on the beach and wait to be rescued. By day they inhabit a land of bright fantastic birds and dark blue seas, but at night their dreams are haunted by the image of a terrifying beast. As the boys' delicate sense of order fades, so their childish dreams are transformed into something more primitive, and their behaviour starts to take on a murderous, savage significance.

ff

The Inheritors

This was a different voice; not the voice of the people.
It was the voice of other.

When the spring came the people moved back to their familiar home. But this year strange things were happening – inexplicable sounds and smells; unexpected acts of violence; and new, unimaginable creatures half glimpsed through the leaves. Seen through the eyes of a small tribe of Neanderthals whose world is hanging in the balance, *The Inheritors* explores the emergence of a new race, *Homo sapiens*, whose growing dominance threatens an entire way of life.

ff

Pincher Martin

Drowning in the freezing North Atlantic, Christopher Hadley Martin, temporary lieutenant, happens upon a grotesque rock, an island that appears only on weather charts. To drink there is a pool of rain water; to eat there are weeds and sea anemones. Through the long hours with only himself to talk to, Martin must try to assemble the truth of his fate, piece by terrible piece. *Pincher Martin* is a terrifying and unforgettable journey into one man's mind.

ff

Free Fall

Somehow, somewhere, Sammy Mountjoy lost his freedom, the faculty of freewill 'that cannot be debated but only experienced, like a colour or the taste of potatoes'. As he retraces his life in an effort to discover why he no longer has the power to choose and decide for himself, the narrative moves between England and a prisoner-of-war camp in Germany. In *Free Fall*, his fourth novel, William Golding has created a poetic fiction, and an allegory, as moving as it is unforgettable.